Summerville Days

Books by Carrie Bender

WHISPERING BROOK SERIES

Whispering Brook Farm
Summerville Days

Miriam's Journal Series

A Fruitful Vine
A Winding Path
A Joyous Heart
A Treasured Friendship

Summerville Days

Carrie Bender

HERALD PRESS
Scottdale, Pennsylvania
Waterloo, Ontario

Library of Congress Cataloging-in-Publication Data
Bender, Carrie, date.
Summerville days / Carrie Bender.
p. cm. — (Whispering brook series)
Summary: When twelve-year-old Mary spends a summer working on her sister's farm in an Amish community, she learns that there is more than one kind of housekeeping.
ISBN 0-8361-9040-8 (alk. paper)
[1. Amish—Fiction. 2. Farm life—Fiction. 3. Family life—Fiction.] I. Title. II. Series.
PZ7.B43136Su 1996
[Fic]—dc20 96-7250
CIP
AC

The paper in this book is recycled and meets the minimum requirements of American National Standard for Information Sciences—Permanence of Paper for Printed Library Materials, ANSI Z39.48-1984.

Scripture quotations are based on the King James Version, adapted toward current English usage. The lines in chap. 5 from E. W. Chapman and A. S. Kieffer are from *Practical Music Reader*. "All work and no play makes Jack a dull boy" is from *Proverbs* (1659), by James Howell. In chap. 14, the chants "I went upstairs," "Mabel, Mabel," and "Sugar, salt" are from *Anna Banana: 101 Jump-Rope Rhymes,* compiled by Joanna Cole (Scholastic, Inc., 1989); permission requested from William Morrow and Company, Inc. In chap. 31, the chorus of the "Good-bye Song" is adapted from *Gospel Country Hymns*, by Lyle Chupp, Shipshewana, Ind.

Library of Congress Catalog Number: 96-7250
International Standard Book Number: 0-8361-9040-8
Printed in the United States of America
Cover art and illustrations by Joy Dunn Keenan
Book design by Paula Johnson

05 04 03 02 01 00 99 98 97 96 10 9 8 7 6 5 4 3 2 1

To all those who wrote letters
to encourage me in my writing,
though I regret I was
unable to answer

Note

This story is fiction,
but true to Amish life.
Any resemblance to persons living
or dead is coincidental.

Contents

1

Bound for Summerville

THE strawberry season was over, and Nancy Petersheim was on her way to Summerville. She was to stay with her sister Mary and brother-in-law Jacob for two whole weeks.

I just hope I won't have an attack of Heemweh (Pennsylvania German for homesickness*),* twelve-year-old Nancy thought as she sat looking out the van window, watching the farms and trees fly by.

Two weeks is a long time to be away from dear Whispering Brook Farm. I'll sure miss Mamm un Daed (Mom and Dad) and the others.

I hope Mary still seems like my sister and not like a Fremdling (stranger). I haven't seen her for four months.

Mary and Jacob had been married the previous fall and moved out of the home community in the spring. Nancy was almost afraid Mary wouldn't seem the same to her.

Nancy's thoughts were interrupted when the van stopped at an Amish farmhouse. A girl about Nancy's age and a boy a year or two older ran out of the house and climbed into the van.

"Hello," said the girl, with a friendly smile on her face. She plopped down on the seat beside Nancy.

Nancy could see that she was sandy-haired, with hazel eyes and a sprinkling of freckles on her tilted-up pug nose.

"I'm Sally Fisher, and this is my brother Andrew." She waved at the boy heading for the back seat. "We were visiting my aunt and uncle for a week, and now we're going home. So, who are you? And where are you going?"

"I'm Nancy Petersheim, and I'm going to Jacob and Mary Yoders' place. Mary's my sister."

Nancy spoke shyly but wanted to be friendly. "They moved to their farm at Summerville in the spring."

"Mary and Jacob Yoder!" Sally cried, her eyes lighting up. "Why, they're our next-door neighbors! Hurrah! I'll get to see a lot of you. How long are you staying?"

"Only two weeks," Nancy replied with regret.

Then she laughed. Just a few minutes ago, she had been thinking that two weeks was a long time. She had wondered if she'd get *Heemweh*, and now already she was saying "only two weeks." This girl certainly was easy to get to know.

"*Ach* (oh) my!" Sally lamented, wrinkling her freckled nose. "I was hoping you'd stay for the summer. I need someone to stick with me against my brother Andrew. He's such a big tease and so *grosshunsich* (smart-alecky). I'd just love to get the best of him sometime."

Nancy chuckled. Sally and her brother sure were characters! She had a feeling there was never a dull moment when they were around.

The van made a few more stops at Amish farms to pick up passengers. Then they were on their way to Summerville, a four-hour drive through the mountains. Soon they were on the turnpike, and Nancy watched the traffic whizzing by.

"Have you ever worked as a *Maut* (helper, hired girl)?" Sally asked.

"No, I haven't," Nancy admitted. "But I figure working for my sister won't be as bad as working for strangers. Besides, Mary probably doesn't have as much work as a mother with lots of little children. She said she wants me to come for a summer vacation."

"So much the better!" Sally cheered the news. "We'll have lots of time together. I'll hurry with my work so Mom will let me come over often.

"Oh, hey, I forgot to tell you that we're getting a Fresh Air girl real soon now, too," Sally bubbled happily. "I can hardly wait."

"Fresh Air girl? What's that?" Nancy was curious.

Sally looked at Nancy as if she were dense. "You mean you've never heard of the Fresh Air program?"

Nancy shook her head. "What is it? Don't you have enough fresh air where you live?"

Sally burst out with giggles. "Of course we do. But the children in the big cities don't have much fresh air. There's all that smoke from the trucks and the factories. So they come out to the country to live on a farm for a two-week vacation.

"They're from low-income families, and the Fresh Air fund pays, so it doesn't cost them anything. Every summer they come by the busload. Our families go to the bus stop if they want a Fresh Air child and are scheduled to host one. There they pick up the child listed for them."

"What if they get homesick and cry?" Nancy wondered. "Can you send them back home?"

Sally shrugged. "They'd soon get over it. My cousins had one last summer, and he really was a spunky little chap. We decided to sign up for a girl this summer, and she's coming in a few days. Ach my, I can hardly wait."

Sally hugged herself in anticipation. "You'll get to see a lot of her, too," she told Nancy. "We'll be over often. My dad has a harness shop, and we don't live on a farm. So she'll want to see cows and other animals that we don't have. We'll bring her over the first day."

"Oh, good! I can hardly wait to see her!" Nancy exclaimed eagerly. "I think it'll be fun to have an *Englischer* (non-Amish) for a friend.

"Oh yes, another thing: I'm having a mystery supper on Sunday evening. I invited a group of girls, and I'm inviting you right now, too."

"Mystery supper? What's that? I've never heard of it."

"Okay, I'll explain. First I'll give the girls a list of all we're having on the menu, and the quantities. Only things won't be called by their right names. The foods might be called names like Slithering Sculpture, Gourmet Garnish, or Ruby Buds. You have to guess what they might be.

"For the first course, you may pick three items. Choose carefully, or you might end up with an odd combination like a heap of spaghetti, a scoop of ice cream, and a knife. Whatever you choose, that's all you get until you've eaten it. Then you get three more choices."

Nancy giggled. "It sounds hilarious. I'm really looking forward to it."

The time passed quickly, with Sally chattering most of the way. Almost before she realized it, the van was stopping at Sally and Andrew's place.

"I'll see you soon," Sally promised as she picked up her travel bags. "Maybe tonight yet—we get our milk at Jacobs'."

She stepped off the van, followed by her brother, who paid the driver. The Fishers' house was comfortable looking, with a vine-shaded porch and a maple tree on either side of the front walk. As Nancy watched, the porch door flew open, and a little girl of about five ran out to greet her brother and sister.

Nancy felt a twinge of *Heemweh*. She wondered what her little sister, Susie, and baby sister, Lydia, were doing at home.

Then they were pulling in at Mary and Jacobs' house, and Nancy was having *Summerflieglis* (butterflies) in her stomach. She had seen their place only once before, but the old red-brick house with two tall pines in front looked homey and familiar.

Nancy quickly paid the driver, picked up her bags, and headed for the house.

Ach my, what if Mary seems like a polite, formal stranger, Nancy worried. *Now she's Mrs. Jacob Yoder, an old married woman. What if things are never the same again, and she doesn't seem like my sister anymore?*

However, Nancy needn't have worried.

2

Cooking for Threshers

"OH, Nancy, are you really here!" cried a voice from the washhouse door. Mary came running out to meet her. She was smiling.

With a feeling of relief, Nancy realized that Mary was still the same sister she always was.

"Do come in!" Mary cried happily. "You're just in time to help me get dinner ready for the threshing crew. The threshing rig came this morning."

Mary was certainly busy. Nancy quickly took her bags upstairs to the room Mary said would be hers. She looked around and saw that the room was cheery. There was a yellow-and-white daisy quilt on the bed, with matching colors on the wallpaper. Plain white nylon curtains hung at the window.

Nancy loved the room at once. She quickly removed her *Schatzli* (little apron), pinned on an everyday one, and hurried downstairs to help Mary.

"Here are some potatoes to peel." Mary came out of the cellarway with a big bowl of potatoes on one arm. Her other arm was clutching several glass jars of fruit. "Tell me all about Mom and Dad and the others as we peel. How are they all?"

"They're fine," Nancy reported. "What do you want to know about them?"

"Well, for one thing, are Joe and Arie still going steady? Are they still a couple?"

"Oh yes," Nancy replied. "He sure thinks a lot of her. Since he's nineteen, I expect they'll be married in a year or two."

"Is Omar dating already?"

"No, he's not. Mom and Dad think he's too young yet, at seventeen, and he's respecting their wishes."

"Tell me all about the others, too. I've been eager for news from the home folks."

"Hmmm, let me think. Dad bought a new work horse last week. Mom got her glasses changed. Steven and Henry have to take turns helping Mom while I'm here. Susie helps wash the breakfast dishes every morning. Pretty good for a six-year-old, don't you think? Baby Lydia is already two and growing fast. She really shouldn't be called a baby anymore."

Mary listened hungrily to each morsel of news about the family at home. She was only twenty-one, and this was her first year of marriage. Although she would never admit it, and least of all to Jacob, she was homesick at times. But having Nancy here would help that.

While preparing the dinner, the sisters chatted as fast as they worked. Finally it was nearly ready. Nancy grated the cabbage for slaw and set the long table. The meat loaf was browned to perfection. Nancy and Mary took turns thumping the big potato masher in the kettle to make *gschtammde Grummbiere* (mashed potatoes).

"Ach my, I almost forgot the washtub!" Mary exclaimed. "There's so many things to do."

She was hot and flustered. This was the first time she was cooking for a crew without her mother's experienced help.

"Quick, Nancy, take this *Bankli* (little bench) out to the yard. We'll put a tub of cool water on it for the men to wash up. Take these clean towels along."

Nancy carried out the bench and washtub, set them under the pump, and laid the towels on the end of the bench. As she pumped water, she watched the men with hayforks pitching the sheaves into the threshing machine.

A few neighbors were already unhitching their horses from the wagons to come for dinner. One team was still in the field being loaded, and others were coming in.

Suddenly Nancy heard someone yelling, and a few men ran toward the wagon in the field. There was a commotion, but then in a few minutes order was restored.

"I wonder what that was all about," Nancy muttered as she hurried back to the house to help Mary put the last-minute touches on the dinner. She dropped an ice cube into each tumbler on the table and filled it with water.

The men came filing into the yard. "Oh look, Mary," Nancy cried. "Andrew Fisher is with the men. I met him and his sister Sally on the van coming here. He must have come over to help as soon as he got home."

Mary looked out the window. "Sure enough, he's here. But I wonder what the men are laughing about.

"Several of the men are clapping Andrew on the back. He must've pulled off another one of his tricks he's so famous for. Oh dear, the men are coming in already! Quick, Nancy, ladle the gravy into the gravy boats. Then stand by the table to keep the *Micke* (flies) off the food."

Jacob's place was at the head of the table. As he walked past Nancy, he tweaked her ear. "I'm glad to see that Mary has help," he welcomed her warmly.

Nancy blushed and smiled back at him. He too, was still the same person, just like when he was Mary's charming beau.

Then out of the corner of her eye, she saw Andrew sit at the table with the other men. He appeared red-faced and quiet, not at all like Sally and Mary had described him. Some of the men were still smiling broadly, as if they could hardly keep a straight face, and Nancy wondered why.

After they all bowed their heads for a silent grace, the eating began.

"Pass the *gschtammde Grummbiere*," Mary told Nancy as she walked by with two platters of meat loaf.

Quickly Nancy passed the mashed potatoes and one dish after the other, as fast as the men were ready for them. It took a lot of food to feed so many hungry hardworking men!

As soon as all the hot foods and other dishes had been passed around the second time, Mary started the desserts. There was chocolate cake, cracker pudding, peaches, and shoofly pie. When the last plate was cleaned, the men bowed their heads again to give thanks to God.

They also thanked Mary for preparing such a good meal as they filed out into the yard to rest in the shade for awhile. By this time, Nancy's stomach was growling hungrily. After all, she hadn't eaten since five o'clock that morning. Mary was out by the water pump, talking with Jacob.

I wish she would hurry back in, so we can eat, Nancy thought impatiently. *She could talk with Jacob some other time.*

At last Mary came in, with news to share. "This time the joke was on Andrew," she chuckled. "I'm sure he didn't feel very cocky then."

"What happened?" Nancy wondered, her curiosity getting the best of her.

"He was forking a sheaf up onto the wagon, and he didn't know there was a snake hiding in it. The snake curled around the handle of his hayfork and slid down, right into his *Latz Hosse* (front flap of his broadfall pants)."

Mary giggled. "Jacob said he jumped right out of his pants faster than he ever got into them! No wonder the men laughed."

Nancy shuddered. *A snake! So there were snakes here in Summerville.*

She tried to laugh with Mary, but inside she was quaking. She was afraid of snakes. *I'll have to watch my step everywhere,* she thought miserably. *Oh well, it'll only be two weeks, and then I'll be at home again, where snakes are rare.*

Mary eyed her keenly. "Are you all right?" she asked.

"That story gives me the shivers," she said. "You know how scared I am of snakes. Poor Andrew!"

However, if Nancy had known what was to happen at Sally's mystery supper, she would have changed her mind about "poor Andrew." Perhaps he deserved that snake, and more!

3

Fresh Air Girl

NANCY soon felt right at home with Mary and Jacob. She and Mary helped Jacob in the dairy barn every morning, and again with the evening milking. That was a job Nancy enjoyed.

They put together the milkers, washed them after the milking was finished, fed the cows, washed their udders, brushed the alleyways with the big push brush, and carried buckets of foaming milk to the milk house. There they poured the milk through filtering funnels into ten-gallon cans.

The Amish don't use high-line electricity, so a diesel engine and generator powered the milkers. Cold mountain spring water was piped down through water troughs to cool the cans of milk.

"I wish we'd have a big dairy like this," Nancy commented to Mary. "Then we'd milk our cows with milkers instead of by hand. Some of your cows are so nice and friendly. I like to pat their noses and talk to them."

"Yes, this is a fine herd. But I wish the cows wouldn't have to be milked on *Sunndaag* (Sunday)," Mary suggested wistfully. "Wouldn't it be nice if cows would hold back their milk on *Sunndaag* and give twice as much on *Moondaag* (Monday)?"

Jacob, passing by with a cart of feed, overheard her and chuckled. "While you're at it, you might as well wish for cows that freshen twice a year, never kick, give hundreds of pounds of milk a day, and never make any piles in the barn."

Nancy giggled.

Mary added, "And let them smell like a rose instead of like a cow. Sally says she can even sniff that *Kiehschmack* (cow smell) in the house, from our chore clothes."

"*Ya, well* (yes, well), I don't care how they *schmack* as long as they make money to pay the bills," declared Jacob. "I couldn't pay off this farm without them."

"In the last *Family Life* magazine," Nancy said, "I read about ant colonies that have herds of insect cows. Of course, they aren't really cows; they're little aphids and scale insects.

"The ants take care of their flocks of cows and tend them, just like the farmer tends the cows. To milk them, they pat the little creatures on the abdomen so they will secrete a delicious sweet milk."

"Whew!" Jacob exclaimed. "No wonder it says in the Bible, 'Go to the ant, thou sluggard.' They must be hardworking little critters."

Nancy heard a shrill whistle from outside.

"That's Sally Fisher, whistling for you," Mary told her. "You're free to go now."

Nancy opened the barn door and stepped out into bright daylight. She blinked her eyes in surprise. There stood Sally, her brother Andrew, little sister Sarah, and the new Fresh Air girl. She was about ten years old, dark-skinned, with many tiny braids all over her head, and wore shorts and a T-shirt.

"Nancy, meet Lakisha Brown, our Fresh Air girl," Sally introduced them with a hint of pride in her voice.

"Hi," Nancy said shyly. "Did you come to see the cows?"

Lakisha nodded. "I saw a cow on TV, and I'd like to see a real one."

Nancy opened the barn door. "Come right on in," she invited.

"The cows are eating breakfast," Andrew told her.

Lakisha stared at the two long rows of cows. "Wow!" was all she managed to say at first. Then she exclaimed "They're huge! What flavor of milk do they give?"

"Well, what flavor would you like?" Andrew teased. "Chocolate, strawberry, or vanilla?"

"No thanks, I'm not hungry now," Lakisha replied politely.

One of the cows raised her tail, and plop, plop,

plop, made a neat pile in the gutter.

"Yuk!" Lakisha held her nose. "Let's get out of here."

"I'll show you the milk house," Nancy offered.

Mary came over to see the city girl. "Hello! Don't you think your parents will miss you while you're away for two whole weeks?"

Lakisha shook her head. "I don't have parents. I live with Nana, my grandma."

"Oh," replied Mary. "Well, I guess she'll be glad to see you when you go home."

"Do you want to see our guinea pigs?" Sally asked Lakisha.

"Pigs? Oink, oink!"

"No, these aren't real pigs; they're guinea pigs. They look more like hamsters or rats," Andrew told her.

"Ugh! Rats!" Lakisha made a face. "We had a rat in our garbage pail behind our apartment building once. I don't think I want to see one."

"Oh no, these are much nicer than rats. Come on. I'll show them to you."

On the way across the yard to the harness shop, Lakisha wondered, "Why did that woman wear such a funny hat on her head, the one like your mom wears, too?"

For a moment Sally looked puzzled, then replied, "Oh, you mean her *Kapp* (cap). That's what all Amish women wear, and little girls wear them only to church. We'll make one for you to wear to church while you're here. Would you like that?"

Lakisha shrugged her shoulders. "That's fine

with me. Will I get to have a horse-and-buggy ride, too?"

"Sure thing," Andrew responded. "Unless you'd rather walk."

Then Nancy had a question for Lakisha. "Who made all your neat little braids? Doesn't that take awfully long?"

"Nana makes them. They only have to be redone several times a year."

The Amish youngsters were as curious about Lakisha's way of living as she was about theirs.

"Here are the guinea pigs," Andrew said, squatting down to the hutch on the grass. "See, their pen doesn't have a bottom. As soon as they've eaten all the grass at one spot, I just move the whole pen. Then they have fresh grass to eat."

"Oh, they're adorable!" Lakisha exclaimed, plopping down on the grass beside them. "Some are brown and white, some are black and white, and some are the same color all over. Will they bite?"

"No, they won't bite," Andrew assured her. "But never lift up a guinea pig by its tail. If you do, its eyes will fall out."

"Honest?" Lakisha didn't believe him. "You're kidding!"

"No, I'm not," Andrew insisted. "It's true!"

Sally got a furry little black-and-white baby out of the pen for Lakisha to hold. "See, guinea pigs don't have tails. You can't lift one up by the tail. Andrew likes to tease."

Lakisha giggled. "Oooh, this one tickles my hand. Put it back in the pen, please."

Five-year-old Sarah reached over, took Lakisha's hand, and spoke up, "*Die hend sin* pink."

"What's she saying?" Lakisha asked. "I don't understand that language."

"She can't talk English yet, so she talks *Deitsch* (Pennsylvania German). She means that the palms of your hands are pink."

"So what?" shrugged Lakisha. "So are the bottoms of my feet. Aren't yours?"

"Would you like to see my *Welschhinkel?*" Andrew suggested.

"Your what? What's a *Velshinkle?*"

"Talk so she can understand, Andrew," Sally scolded. "He means a turkey—here in the pen."

"Oh, gobble, gobble," Lakisha tried to talk turkey. "Every year at Thanksgiving, a church gives us a free turkey, ready to roast."

The door to the screened porch opened, and Mom Fisher called out, "Sally, will you bring me some *Seisswelschkann Kolwe* out of the garden, for dinner? The patch that we had under plastic is ready. Andrew, you're to go help Dad in the harness shop."

"What's that *Velsh?*" Lakisha wondered. "Is that something like a turkey, too?"

"Sweet corn!" Sally exclaimed. "The first of the season! Let's go get some right here in the garden. I can hardly wait to eat a roasting ear."

"We buy our corn at the supermarket," Lakisha said. "I didn't know they grow on stalks like this."

"It's so much better fresh out of the garden," Sally told her. She tore an ear of corn down and off the stalk. "Here, hold out your aprons," she directed the girls. "I'll take the *Bascht* off, and you can carry the ears in your aprons."

"Now you're doing it too," Lakisha complained. "How am I supposed to know what *Basht* is?"

"Oh, you're right. Sometimes I can't think of the English word right away. I meant the husks."

Sally began putting cleaned ears of corn into Nancy's and Sarah's aprons.

"I want an apron, too," pouted Lakisha. "I can't carry much corn in my T-shirt."

"You'll get one before Sunday," Sally promised. "Mom is going to make you an Amish dress and apron for church. Would you like that?"

"I sure would. And I'd like to go barefoot too, like you do."

"You'd better not! You might step on a bee and get stung. That hurts. Just keep on wearing your sandals. Tonight after sundown, when the bees fly away to sleep, you can go barefoot in the grass."

They took the corn into the kitchen. "Mom, may we take Lakisha for a pony ride before lunch?" Sally asked.

Mom Fisher was rolling out dough for pies. "I'm making raisin pies, and I just discovered that I'm out of clear jell. I can't thicken pies without clear jell. So why don't you drive to the Four Corners Bulk Food Store and get me some? I'll make a list for you since I need a few other things, too."

"Let's go!" Sally was eager to show off the pony and cart. She slipped Mom's list and money into a dress pocket and raced outside with the other girls.

Nancy pulled the little spring wagon out of the

shed, and Sally threw the harness on the pony's back and buckled it tight.

"How fast can your pony go?" Lakisha wondered. "As fast as a subway?"

"What's a subway?" Sally wondered back. "Do you mean a sandwich or a submarine?"

Lakisha hooted with laughter. "A subway is a train under the ground," she explained. "There are lots of them in New York City."

"Why would anyone want to bury a train?" Sally asked. "What good would it do down there?"

"You're gross," Lakisha groaned. "Aye-mish people must be dumb!"

"Well, then, so are you!" Sally replied. "You thought a cow would give flavored milk. Ei yi yi!"

Suddenly both girls began to giggle.

"I guess I'm just as dumb about things here in the country as you are about things in the city," Lakisha admitted. "Let's be friends, anyway."

"Yes, let's!" Sally agreed. "You can sit on the front seat beside me and Nancy, and Sarah can sit on the wagon bed behind us.

"Now, hang on! Giddap, Maggie!" She slapped the lines on the pony's back, and she started off with a brisk trot.

"Hey, this is fun!" Lakisha cried. "I'm glad I'm here. This is better than watching TV!"

Sarah leaned over and whispered to Nancy, "*Die schwatz Meedel gleicht pony Faahre* (the black girl likes a pony ride)."

Nancy nodded. "*Ich gleich es aa* (I like it, too)."

4

The Mystery Supper

IT was Sunday evening, and Nancy was on her way to Sally Fisher's mystery supper. She felt a little nervous about meeting Sally's chums—so many girls she'd never met before.

Today had been this district's in-between (no-church) Sunday, so she hadn't even had a chance to meet any of them at the preaching services. Would she stand in the corner all evening feeling out of place, or would Sally make sure she felt like one of them?

Nancy wished she wouldn't be quite so shy. It would be much easier to make new friends if she were more outgoing. She found it difficult to think of those first words to say to start talking with strangers. But Sally sure was friendly, so maybe things would work out all right.

A robin sang from the walnut tree beside the road. In Jacob's meadow, the cows were heading to the barn to be milked. It was a pleasant, not-so-hot evening. Nancy forgot her fears and looked forward eagerly to the evening. She had never before been to a mystery supper, and it was bound to be lots of fun.

Nancy opened the Fishers' kitchen door and stepped inside without knocking, in the Amish custom.

"Come right in," Sally called happily. "You're the first one here, and I could use some help in preparing supper. Mom and Dad and Lakisha and Sarah went to Uncle Eli's for supper, so I have to get the meal ready alone.

"Andrew's here yet, and he keeps bothering me so much that I can't think straight. Why don't you scat, Andrew?" Sally scolded her brother as he snitched a piece of candy from the dish on the table. "*Geh badder die Katz* (go bother the cat)."

"Oh, hello," Andy said politely to Nancy, ignoring his sister. "I heard something about you the other day, that you're scared of snakes! Well, well, I'll have to cure you of that sometime. I know just what would do it."

Sally grabbed the broom from behind the range and ran toward Andrew with it. "How dare you tease my company like that!" she sputtered. "*Nau geh naus!* (now get out of here)."

Andrew fled, crying "Help, help, somebody help me!" as he ran out to the barn.

"I don't know what ails him today," Sally muttered. "Maybe it's because so many girls are coming."

Nancy felt mortified. Who would've told Andrew that she was afraid of snakes? Did Mary tell Jacob, and Jacob told one of the threshers, and Andrew overheard? Oh well, it didn't matter? Andrew was just a big tease, and Nancy determined that she would not mind him.

"I wish Lakisha were here," Sally said wistfully. "She'd be the life of the party. I can just hear the girls make a fuss over her.

"Oh, here comes a group of them now. Come right in, girls," she called out to the porch. "Come and meet Nancy Petersheim. She's staying with her sister, Mary, and Jacob Yoder."

Though Sally introduced the smiling, friendly girls to Nancy, the names didn't mean much to her yet. They were all dressed alike with their hair neatly combed back under a white *Kapp*. Each wore a dark solid-colored *Rock* (dress) with a white *Schatz* (apron).

"Come into the *Sitzschtupp* (sitting room) while Nancy and I get supper ready," Sally invited them. "You aren't allowed to see what we're preparing, and even Nancy won't get to see the names on the menu."

Sally's mother had prepared several different casseroles and side dishes, and all Sally had to do was heat them in the gas oven. In the gas refrigerator were several elaborately prepared desserts.

Andrew came back into the kitchen. "I'll be good

now. Won't you let me help?" he wheedled.

"*Wann du dich schickscht* (if you behave)," Sally replied. "We sure could use your help, since you already know the names of the dishes. I don't want Nancy to miss out on any of the fun."

Andrew grabbed an apron that was hanging on a hook behind the kitchen range and wrapped it around himself, tying it in the back. He pretended to be dancing a jig, swinging jauntily from side to side. He began to chant,

> Now you'll see,
> Tee hee hee,
> That Andy can cook,
> Without a cookbook.

Nancy couldn't help but laugh. Andrew was so comical.

But Sally didn't think it was funny. "*Schick dich!* (behave)," she said sharply, "*odder geh naus!* (or get out)."

To Nancy she confided, "Isn't he a pain in the neck?"

Finally Sally managed to get Andy started in making a tossed salad.

"Here are the menu sheets," she told Nancy. "Put one at each plate. Then call the girls to the table."

A bit shyly, Nancy went to the door of the *Sitzschtupp*. "Supper's ready," she announced.

The girls didn't have to be told twice. They hungrily scanned the menu and chattered about what they would order.

"Fisherman's Gold!" exclaimed a girl named Barbie, sitting on Nancy's right. "I guess we'll all be rich if we can pull in the fish. And Shimmering Sauce! What could that be?"

"Snow on the Mountain," said another girl. "How are we supposed to know whether that's *gschtammde Grummbiere* (mashed potatoes) or ice cream?"

"Galloping Gixer! That's got to be a fork."

"Scalloped Splender, Bald Eagle Hash! Ugh!"

Nancy had been right. It was hilarious. The first girl to order received a plate, a serving of salad, a mound of vanilla pudding, some gravy, and only a knife with which to eat it. Amidst cheers and groans, she did her best. At least it wasn't as bad as trying to eat with chopsticks.

Some fared a little better, but others had even worse combinations. Nancy was the last to order. She chose Italian Idiocracy, Elegant Entrée, and Supreme Surprise. When Andrew brought the plate to the table, it was covered by an upside-down dish. With a flourish he set it down in front of her.

"Something extra for the new girl," he announced loudly. "She deserves a special serving."

Nancy felt embarrassed as all eyes turned toward her. None of the other girls had gotten a covered plate.

Carefully she lifted the dish. "Oooh, *en Shlang!* (a snake)," she screamed at the top of her lungs. She scrambled away from the table so fast that her chair overturned.

Pandemonium broke loose as the shrieking girls

cleared out, trying to get away from the curled-up snake on Nancy's plate.

"Andrew, *du Dummkopp!* (you dunce)," Sally cried. "You've ruined our supper."

This time she grabbed the broom in earnest and advanced menacingly upon him. Andrew, seeing the dire straits he was in, grabbed the rubber snake, stuffed it in his pocket, and hightailed it out the door.

Nancy was trembling. She had seen what she thought was a real live snake, right in front of her on her plate. It was too much. She knew she was too unnerved to eat a bite now.

"That terrible Andrew!" Sally complained, close to tears. "Let's plan something to get even with him. He ought to be whipped. I'll ask Dad tonight to get a switch and *bletsch* (spank) him!"

All evening they plotted together, thinking up ways to get even with Andrew, but finally gave it up.

"*Brutzing* (pouting) like this won't help," Barbie finally proposed. "Attention is just what he wants anyway. So let's just ignore him."

The girls all agreed: That would be best.

5

A Picnic

MARY was not as busy anymore, now that the threshing was done. She decided to plan for an outing.

"Let's take our supper down to the creek tonight, after the milking is done, and have a picnic, the way we used to at home along Whispering Brook," Mary proposed to Nancy on Tuesday morning. "I remember how much you used to like that."

"Well, I guess that would be all right." She wasn't as enthused about the prospect as Mary thought she would be.

Nancy didn't want to admit to Mary that she was afraid there would be snakes along the creek. Summerville was close to the wild mountains. For all she knew, there might be poisonous snakes here, such as rattlesnakes, copperheads, and water moccasins.

Nancy shuddered. Sunday evening's fright certainly hadn't cured her of her fear. It only made it worse.

"Don't you want to go picnicking, Nancy?" Mary quizzed her in surprise. "I was so sure you'd like it that I already invited Sally and Andrew and the Fresh Air girl. They're bringing marshmallows to toast."

"That should be fun." Nancy spoke brightly and tried to sound convincing.

Yet she was thinking, *Andrew will be sure to bring that rubber snake in his pocket and will chase me with it. Oh well, I'll just pretend I'm not the least bit afraid. Then it won't be fun for him to tease me.*

After settling that in her mind, Nancy felt better. She tried to sound casual as she asked, "Are there any poisonous snakes around here?"

Mary laughed. "Now I understand. I was worrying that maybe you were getting a bad case of *Heemweh*. I knew something was wrong when you were not jumping up and down, eager to go for a picnic.

"No, I can assure you, there are no *gifdich Schlange* (poisonous snakes) around here."

"I'm glad," Nancy said. "Now I can look forward to tonight."

She vigorously stirred the cookie dough. Tuesday was baking day at Mary's house. In the afternoon they made half-moon pies and finger cakes to take along to the picnic. Then before they went to do the chores, they made cheese-and-lettuce sandwiches. They wrapped all the prepared food and put it in the picnic basket.

As soon as the chores were finished, Sally, Andrew, Sarah, and Lakisha came over to join them. The merry little group traipsed down through the meadow, searching for the ideal picnic spot.

"You youngsters can gather twigs and small dead branches for firewood," Jacob told them. "We'll build a cozy little fire to keep the bears away."

"Bears!" Lakisha exclaimed. "You gotta be kiddin'!"

"He is," Mary assured her. "There are a few black bears in the mountains, but not on the farms. Only raccoons and muskrats and woodchucks, and little animals like bunnies, chipmunks, squirrels, and a few foxes."

"Where are they now?" Lakisha asked, looking around half fearfully.

"They're all hidden away in their dens and nests, waiting until after dark to come out," Mary told her. "They're afraid of us. After we go home, they'll come around and eat the crumbs we leave."

Nancy spread the tablecloth on the grass. She could hardly believe how different Lakisha looked tonight. She was wearing an Amish dress and apron instead of those little shorts that showed her bare brown legs. Except for her dark skin and those many little braids, she looked like a little Amish *Meedel* (girl.)

When the fire was blazing cheerfully, Jacob and Andrew used their pocketknives to cut long, sturdy twigs off the trees. They sharpened the ends and stripped off bark to make sticks for spearing the hot dogs and roasting them over the fire.

"Where are the rolls for the hot dogs?" Lakisha wondered.

"We don't have any. We just use homemade bread," Mary explained. She took the bread knife and began to slice the bread. "There are sandwiches, too. You could just slip your hot dog inside a sandwich."

"Oh, gross!" Lakisha muttered, rolling her eyes. "You guys are weird."

Andy snorted in disgust and told the others, "*Ach mei, sie denkt alles is gross, un sie wisst net ewe das* gross *meent* big *in Deitsch* (oh my, she thinks everything is gross, and she doesn't even know that *gross* means *big* in German)."

Mary quickly set him straight. "If you'd visit New York City, you might think some things there seem gross, too. Now please speak only in English so Lakisha doesn't feel left out."

"Okay, we're ready to start." She beckoned to her husband.

Jacob joined the circle and said solemnly, "Let's ask the blessing."

All bowed their heads and closed their eyes for a few moments in silent thanksgiving to God for life, food, and fun.

"Okay, now dig in," Jacob invited everyone. "The doggies are browned just right."

"Why do you always bow your heads before you eat?" Lakisha wondered.

"Don't you ask a blessing or say thanks before you eat at home?" asked Sally.

"No. We don't even sit down together to eat," Lakisha replied. "We just have a snack whenever we're hungry. Nana hardly ever cooks."

"Well, no wonder you never eat much at mealtimes, then ask for a snack soon after the meal," Andrew griped. "If you'd eat enough at mealtimes, you wouldn't need to eat between meals."

"Now, now, let's not judge each other," Jacob reproved mildly. "Andy, I've never seen you turn down a cookie anytime, day or night."

They all chuckled and relaxed. Jacob added, "When we're finished eating, we can sing a few songs. And maybe Lakisha can sing a solo for us."

It was a lovely and peaceful evening. As dusk was settling over the countryside, night insects began their evening chorus. An owl hooted from a tree in the meadow, and frogs began to croak from a nearby pool, in low and poignant tones.

The dear, familiar sounds reminded Nancy of Whispering Brook Farm and filled her heart with peace and contentment. But Lakisha clapped her hands over her ears. To her, the noises were weird and annoying.

Nancy found herself wondering what life would be like in the middle of New York City, with only a grandmother for a family, and spending most of her time watching TV. No green grass, trees, flowers, gardens, birds, farm animals, and creeks.

Suddenly Lakisha jumped up. "What are those little flying lights?" She slapped her hands together and caught one.

"Fireflies," Sally told her. "Haven't you ever seen

fireflies before? Imagine that!"

Lakisha was delighted. "May I catch as many as I want? I'd like to take some along home to show Nana."

"I don't think they'd like it in the city," Mary said, chuckling. "Maybe you'd better leave them here."

When the children tired of chasing fireflies, Mary and Jacob sang a few German songs and explained them to Lakisha.

Then Nancy urged, "Let's sing the 'Honeycup' song. I like that one."

Jacob began it, and the others joined in.

> There are bright tinted flowers
> Where the soft breezes float,
> And the dews of the evening fall,
> Where the bird and the bee
> From the honeycups drink,
> For the sun shineth bright over all. . . .
> 'Tis a beautiful earth,
> With it's brilliance and shade,
> For the sun shineth bright over all.
>
> —*E. W. Chapman*

Nancy's heart throbbed as the last note died away. *It's so beautiful*, she thought.

"Now sing 'Twilight Is Stealing' yet," Andrew suggested. "That's the one I like best."

"Start it," Jacob replied. "We'll pitch in."

Andrew led out in a shaky voice, and the others joined him.

Twilight is stealing over the sea,
Shadows are falling dark on the lea.
Borne on the night winds voices of yore
Come from that far-off shore.
Far away, beyond the starlit skies,
Where the love light never, never dies,
Gleameth a mansion filled with delight,
Sweet happy home so bright.

—A. S. Kieffer

"Your songs give me thrills and chills," Lakisha said. "They make me want to cry."

Sally stirred up the fire. "Time to toast marshmallows," she announced, spearing two on a stick.

"Lakisha didn't sing her solo yet," Jacob teased.

"Oh, all right, I'll sing one that Nana taught me." Lakisha sang in a low, throaty voice.

Down by de cane brake, close by de mill,
Dar lived a lil darkie gal, her name was Bessie Bill.
In a town close by where Bessie Bill did dwell,
Dar lived a boy dat courted her.
She loved him quite well.

"Ouch!" cried Lakisha, slapping her arm. "Something is stinging my arms and buzzing in my ears."

"Mosquitoes!" Jacob declared. "Finish toasting those marshmallows, and then we'll go inside."

"Finish your song first," Andrew prodded. "I'd like to hear the rest of it."

"I can't remember the rest of it. Anyhow, I don't like mosquitoes. Let's go."

"Okay, gather up the tablecloth and the wrappers," Mary told the girls. "Andrew can help Jacob outen the fire."

As they trudged through the meadow toward the house, Andrew fell into step beside Nancy and commented in a low voice, "Black songs are quite different from ours, aren't they?"

Nancy nodded. "But she has a good voice for singing."

"Nancy, would you like to go along to catch pigeons in Aquila Riehl's barn some evening?" he asked. "Sally wants to go, and if you want to, you're welcome to come along."

"I think I'd like that," Nancy agreed. "That is, if Mary and Jacob don't care."

Jacob overheard and spoke up, "I don't mind, if you'll be careful about not falling down hay holes and not climbing dangerously high."

So the pigeon hunt was planned for Friday evening. Nancy promised to watch out for holes in the barn floor through which hay was thrown down into the stable for the cows and horses.

As she prepared for bed, Nancy mused, *Andrew was nice tonight. Maybe he wanted to make up for teasing me with that snake.*

6

Showing Off

ON Wednesday morning Mary asked, "How would you like to go along to a quilting at Abe's Jakie's today? Jacob said I could drive King. There are always plenty of *Buppelin* (babies) there to cuddle while the mothers quilt."

"I'd like that" Nancy agreed. "I really miss little Lydia. She's such a *Leibschdi* (sweetheart)."

So they quickly washed the dishes and swept the kitchen. Mary prepared a casserole for Jacob's lunch.

"Be sure to watch King if another horse tries to pass," Jacob reminded Mary, as she and Nancy got onto the buggy. "That's when he holds hard and tries to race or even run away. Keep a good grip on the reins and pull back."

"I will," Mary promised. "If I don't let him speed up at all, I don't think I'll have any problems."

It was a beautiful morning, and King trotted down the road in brisk and upheaded style. Morning mists hung over the fields and sparkled in the sunshine.

Nancy took a deep breath. "Oh, I just love to go driving in the morning when all is still clean and fresh and dewy." She was full of rapture. "I could just breathe in great gulps of that fresh scented air."

"I know," Mary agreed, "at least on this country back road. But we'll soon be out on the highway. Then I'll have to keep a constant eye on the traffic, and I won't be able to enjoy the scenery much."

Nancy perked up her ears. Behind her there was a fast staccato of hoofbeats on the pavement. She looked back. "There comes Andrew on the pony spring wagon!" she informed Mary. "And he's coming fast. I think he'll try to pass."

"He'd better not pass now," Mary said sharply. "There's a car coming up ahead."

"He *is* passing, though!" Nancy cried. "And he's tapping the pony with the whip to make her go faster."

Mary was trying to rein King in, but the pony excited him, and he began to gallop. The two rigs were side by side now. To beat the car that was coming toward them, Andrew lashed Maggie to make her go faster.

The pony lunged ahead, and at that moment the spring wagon seat tilted backward and dumped Andrew on his back in the wagon bed.

Mary and Nancy stared openmouthed to see Andrew there on his back with his legs waving straight up in the air, still holding unto the reins. In a moment Andrew was up again, yanking on the reins to stop the pony.

The car had pulled off to the side of the road and stopped. "Are you all right?" the driver of the car asked Andrew.

By this time he had slowed the pony to a stop. Mary had also brought King to a standstill, though he was still restless.

"Y-yes, I th-think so," stammered Andrew shamefacedly.

"You can't drive lying on your back, can you?" the man teased him, laughing good-naturedly.

Andrew's face reddened, and he mumbled, "That seat was taken off to haul something big. Then it wasn't screwed fast again when it was replaced." Andrew didn't feel like admitting that he himself had forgotten to bolt the seat down.

King was snorting and impatient to be off, so Mary drove away.

"I hope that taught Andrew a lesson," Mary remarked. "He thinks racing is smart. What if that car would've been going too fast to stop? He's a *wunderbaar* (terrible) show-off. But I guess, lying on the wagon, he sure wasn't *grossfiehlich* (feeling important) then."

After another mile, Mary observed, "Well, here we are at Abe's Jakie's." She guided King in the lane. "Look at all those buggies. I hope we're not late."

"Hurrah!" Nancy suddenly shouted. "There in

the yard are Sally and Lakisha! I didn't expect to see them here."

"Help me unhitch first, before you run off," Mary urged. "Hand me the halter."

When King was tied in the barn, Nancy joined the other girls.

"Hi, Clancy!" Lakisha greeted her, smiling.

Sally giggled. "It's Nancy," she corrected.

"Ooops, I goofed. Sorry!" Lakisha apologized.

Nancy gave her a friendly smile. "What do you think your grandma would say if she could see you dressed like an Amish girl?"

Lakisha giggled. "Boy, would I like to see her face! I wish you people would have cameras, so I could show her a picture."

"Well, we don't," Sally said practically. "Let's go look at the quilts, then find ourselves some *schnuck Buppelin* to hold."

"What are *schnuck Buppelin?*" Lakisha asked.

"Cute babies!" Sally told her. "Don't you like to hold babies? They're so sweet and cuddly."

"I never held one. I wouldn't know how."

Nancy and Sally exchanged glances. "Imagine that!" Sally exclaimed. "You never held a baby? You've missed half your life! It's about time you learn."

"Hey! Look at that horse." Lakisha pointed to a horse tied to a fence out back of the barn. "He's an angry beast, pawing the ground like that."

The girls stopped to watch. The horse was hitched to a two-wheeled cart.

"He is acting mighty impatient," Sally agreed. "I

wonder what ails him?"

"Look!" Nancy cried. "He's tied too close to a beehive. No wonder he's pawing. The bees are coming out."

"Uh, oh, he knocked the beehive over, and lots more bees are pouring out," Sally cried in alarm. "*Spring* (run) and tell the men."

But the three girls stood rooted to the spot, unable to move.

"*Der Gaul is um los reisse!* (the horse is going to tear loose)," Nancy cried.

He was throwing himself backward, straining on the neck rope. Suddenly the rope snapped in two, and the horse took off down the field with the cart bumping along behind him.

"Help! Help! Help! Help!" Lakisha hollered shrilly, at the top of her lungs. "Somebody help quick! The bees are after the horse, and he's running away!"

Abe's Jakie and his sons came running out of the barn. Nancy pointed to the runaway horse. "The bees are after him!" she cried.

Lakisha kept on yelling and yelling as loud as she could.

"Stop it!" Sally scolded. "Lakisha, yelling won't help anything now anymore. Be quiet! You're bursting my eardrums. The men will catch him."

But Lakisha continued yelling and yelling.

"Stop it! I said," Sally cried. She clapped her hand over Lakisha's mouth. "Save your voice!

"Once a woman yelled so loud when her man's horses ran away that she lost her voice completely and couldn't talk for two years! She could only whisper all that time. You wouldn't want that to happen to you, would you?"

Finally Lakisha quieted down. Jakie and his boys each saddled a horse and soon caught the runaway. The bees returned to their hive.

"Ach my, I feel so sorry for the poor horse," Nancy moaned. "He probably got a lot of stings. I hope he'll be all right."

"What does a bee sting feel like?" Lakisha wondered. "Like an injection?"

"Just be glad you don't know," Sally told her. "The itching and the swelling afterward is worse than the sting."

The girls went to see the four beautiful quilts in the frames in Jakie's big shop. They were in time for the cookies and apple *Schnitz* (slices) and bananas being passed around for a forenoon snack.

"Why does everyone stare at me so?" Lakisha muttered. "I don't like that."

"Just ignore it," Sally whispered. "They all want to see what an Amish-dressed Fresh Air girl from New York City looks like. When we get to the city, people stare at us, too. We just look the other way."

The girls went back outside to see the stung horse. Jakie and the boys had tied him under the overhang of the barn and were dousing him with water from a hose.

"How is he?" Lakisha asked. "Is he going to die?"

"No, I think he'll be all right," Jakie answered. "It's a good thing he tore loose and ran away, though, or they might've killed him. I never once thought about it that someone might tie a horse there. Whoever it was must have thought the hive was empty."

"I'm powerful glad the horse is okay," Lakisha exclaimed. "All right, now where are the papooses?"

Sally giggled. "If you mean the *schnuck Buppelin* (cute babies), come and I'll show you."

The girls ran happily to the house.

7

The Accident

NANCY did not get to go pigeon hunting with Andrew and Sally on Friday evening after all. On Friday morning she and Mary worked in the garden, pulling weeds from the rows. Then Jacob came with King hitched to the *Schaufeleeg* (cultivator), ready to work up the soil between the rows.

"Can you lead King?" Jacob asked Mary. "He has never been ridden. If he had, I'd let Nancy ride him while I *schaufle* (cultivate)."

"I wish you'd have hitched one of the steady old workhorses," Mary said. "King is so *schusslich* (careless, rushing). I'm afraid he'll step on my foot."

"If you're willing to wait till tomorrow to have this job done, I'll use one of the workhorses," Jacob told her. "Yes, that would be better. Remember, Andrew borrowed the workhorses to haul manure out of their barn today."

"No, let's do it now," Mary objected. "I'd like to have the garden *gschaufelt* today, if possible. It looks for rain, and if we don't get it done before it rains, I'm afraid the weeds will get the best of us. I think I can handle King."

Up and down the rows they went, Mary leading King and Jacob manning the cultivator with both hands. Soon the garden was nearly finished.

Suddenly Mary yelled, "Ouch, ouch, my leg!" She let go of King's bridle and sank to the ground.

Jacob quickly grabbed the reins hanging on the handles of the cultivator and stopped King. "Did King step on your foot?" he asked anxiously, hurrying to her side.

"No, I stepped against a sharp stake!" Mary moaned. "It's still jabbed into my leg."

Nancy took one look at Mary's injured leg and turned pale.

"*Mach schnell* (hurry), Nancy, run to the Fishers and tell them to get someone to take Mary to the doctor!" Jacob cried. "There's a telephone behind their harness shop."

Nancy ran, as fast as she could, until her breath came in sharp gasps and her side ached. Sally met her at the door.

"*Was is letz* (what's wrong)?" she wondered in alarm. "Is anyone hurt?"

Nancy nodded, still gasping too much to talk. Finally she found her voice.

"Call the doctor, er—I mean, call someone to take Mary to the doctor. She stepped on a sharp stake in the garden, and it's still poking into her leg!"

Without another word, Sally ran to tell Dad Fisher, in the harness shop. He went to the nearest *englisch* neighbor's place. A short time later, kindhearted Mrs. Davis drove up in her car, and Nancy got in.

"How bad is it?" Mrs. Davis wondered. "Maybe it would be better to call an ambulance."

"No, I don't think it's that bad. Not if you get her to the doctor right away." Nancy was worried about Mary, but she knew they didn't want the extra expense of an ambulance unless it was necessary.

In a few moments, they drove in the lane to the garden. Jacob had pulled the stake out of Mary's leg and hastily wrapped the wound. Now he carried Mary to the car.

"You can stay here, Nancy," he told her. "Maybe you can have dinner ready by the time we get back."

Nancy nodded mutely. It was hard to see Mary in pain like that, and tears pushed from her eyes. After they left, she went into the kitchen and opened the refrigerator door. There were some leftovers and a dish of fresh black raspberries.

Maybe I can make some cold berry soup, Nancy planned. *That will be quick and easy.*

She went out to work at weeding the garden rows again. Near noon, she washed her dirty hands at the outdoor pump, then went into the kitchen to get dinner ready. The kitchen felt nice and cool after working in the hot sun.

Nancy broke four slices of bread into small pieces in a glass dish, added the sweetened raspberries, and poured milk over it all. The milk turned pale lavender from the raspberries. She took the roll of home-cured bologna from the refrigerator and sliced off a few pieces to make sandwiches.

There was the sound of a car in the drive, and Nancy looked out the window. Yes, it was Mrs. Davis' car, and Jacob was carrying Mary into the house. Her leg was carefully bandaged, and he laid her on the kitchen couch.

"Well, Nancy," he said, "it looks as if you'll have to stay longer than you planned. The doctor says Mary has to stay off her feet for quite awhile."

"Oh!" was all Nancy managed to say. She had never once thought of that.

"Are you willing to stay longer?" Mary asked. "Or would that upset you?"

"No, I'll stay," Nancy promised quickly, hoping her voice sounded convincing and trying to smile. "I do like to work for you."

"All right, then. Please bring me a paper and pencil, and I'll write a note to Mom before the mail carrier goes."

"Well, at least I'll have a good cook then," Jacob joked. "This berry soup does look good."

After the dishes were washed and Mary was resting in the bedroom, Nancy decided to make some cherry *Gnepplin* (dumplings).

She thought, *I'd better start right now, so they'll be ready in time for supper. Grandma used to say, "As long as it gives Gnepplin and cabbage, the Deitsch-*

mann (dutchman) will not die."

First she got a can of sour cherries from the cellar and thickened them with clear jell. Then she mixed the flour, eggs, and milk. She stirred them until a smooth batter was formed, then dropped the batter, a teaspoon at a time, into boiling water.

Now let that boil for a few minutes, Nancy told herself. She went outside to sit on the porch glider to cool off.

"Yahoo, Nancy," called a voice from the road. Sally and Lakisha were in the spring wagon, pulled by the pony. "Come along for a ride," Sally called, motioning to Nancy.

Forgetting all about her *Gnepplin,* Nancy dashed out to the pony and hopped up on the seat beside the girls.

"Giddap, Maggie!" yelled Sally, and off they went.

"Wow! This pony can sure run!" Lakisha chattered. "No wonder Andrew likes to race with her."

Suddenly Nancy remembered the loose seat. "Sally, has this seat been fastened?" she asked anxiously.

"Why, yes," Sally replied. "Andrew had the seat off to haul some bales of hay, but he bolted it fast again before we started out. What made you think about that? You're not a worrywart, are you?"

Nancy laughed. "I hope not." Just then she decided not to tell Sally about Andrew's tumble. What if she had been the one who fell over backward while driving the pony? The fewer the people who found it out, the better she would feel.

A strong south wind was blowing, and Nancy relaxed, enjoying the swish of the wind on her face. It gave her a feeling of exhilaration.

Lakisha felt it, too, and exclaimed happily, "This is so much fun! It feels almost like flying! I wish we could ride the rest of the day."

They went around what they called their square mile, then Sally said, "Well, I guess we have to get home and pick string beans for supper." She reined the pony to a stop in front of Mary and Jacob's house.

"Thanks for the ride," Nancy called, then ran happily to the house.

Even before she reached the porch, she smelled it. *Ach my, what's that awful odor?* she wondered. "Oh no, my *Gnepplin!*" she moaned.

As she dashed into the house, Mary called from the bedroom, "Nancy, is something burning?"

"I'll take care of it!" Nancy yelled back. She grabbed a potholder and ran outside with the burned black kettle. *What can I do with this awful mess?* she thought wildly.

Then she had a bright idea. She ran into the woodshed, grabbed a shovel, and furiously began to dig a hole in the garden. Quickly she scraped the dried and burned *Gnepplin* into the hole and began to cover them with dirt.

Suddenly she heard a snicker behind her and whirled around. There stood Andrew by the lane fence, laughing at her, obviously enjoying her plight.

"What?" he drawled. "You weren't trying to fry a snake, were you?" He laughed uproariously at his own joke, then sauntered off.

Andrew called back over his shoulder, "We're not going pigeon hunting till next Friday."

Nancy didn't answer. *That Andrew!* she thought unhappily. *Now he'll tell everyone what I did, and he'll tease me mercilessly about it every time he sees me. Sally sure was right. He is a pain in the neck!*

8

A Prank in Church

IT was Sunday morning, and Nancy and Jacob were getting ready to go to church at Sol Bylers' place. Mary had to stay at home because of her leg but had urged Nancy to go with Jacob.

"I guess people will wonder whether I've taken a new wife," Jacob teased as Nancy sat on the buggy seat beside him and King pranced out the lane.

Nancy blushed. "Ach no!" she protested indignantly, then wondered why Jacob laughed so heartily.

At Sol Bylers', benches had been set up in the large shop for the church services. Nancy sat beside Sally and listened to the familiar old slow tunes. Jacob was a *Vorsinger* (song leader), and his rich baritone voice rose and fell in a solo until it was time for the others to join in.

Nancy did not know the preachers here in Summerville. The preacher who had the *Aafang* (shorter beginning sermon) spoke in a singsong way that made her feel sleepy, and her thoughts began to wander.

Across the shop, she spied Andrew sitting with bowed head. Her thoughts drifted back to last evening, when she had been in Jacob's milk house, washing the milkers, and Andrew had come in with his gallon jug for milk.

"Hey, Nancy," he had started, trying to sound cool. "I just thought I'd let you know that I didn't tell anyone how you were digging for snakes in the garden yesterday."

Quickly Nancy had looked at Andrew to see if he was teasing. She decided that he meant what he said about not telling. Yet he surely was kidding about digging for snakes. He had rolled his eyes, but his voice had been kind.

Nancy understood. Andrew wanted to assure her that he wasn't going to pass around a story of seeing her in the garden, burying a flop—burned food. To cover his awkwardness, he had kept up his pretense that she was digging for snakes.

Now she was sure of it: Andrew had a good heart. His *grosshunsich* (smart-alecky) ways and show-off actions must be just a cover-up for other feelings. Suddenly she was glad she hadn't told Sally about Andrew's embarrassing flip while racing with the pony and wagon.

Shyly Nancy had replied to Andrew in the milk house, "Neither did I tell anyone about the tumble you took on the spring wagon!"

Andrew had grinned his thanks and gone on his way, whistling a happy tune.

Abruptly Nancy was awakened out of her daydreaming by something the preacher was saying. What had caught her attention? Was the preacher talking about snakes now, too?

He was saying, "The seed of the serpent and the seed of the woman have been enemies to each other ever since the snake deceived Eve in the garden of Eden.

"People have a natural fear of the snake, because God created us that way. You can read about snake charmers and snake handlers in the papers. But I don't believe that's the way God intended us to be. It's natural to be afraid of snakes."

Nancy heaved a sigh of relief. At least this preacher was on her side. She hoped Andrew was listening and wouldn't tease her about snakes any more. She had a feeling he wouldn't.

Nancy felt herself getting drowsy again. My, it was warm! The shop doors were wide open, but hardly a breeze stirred. A bee buzzed in and droned lazily at the window. Nancy glanced over to the bench where Lakisha was sitting. She wondered how the Fresh Air girl was taking it, having to sit still so long.

Lakisha was not used to going to church at all. And now she couldn't understand a word of what was going on. *How would I feel if I'd be in New York*

City, sitting in a church full of blacks? Nancy wondered.

Suddenly she felt a surge of respect for Lakisha. *What a brave girl she must be! If it would be me, I'd have a bad case of Heemweh (homesickness).*

Sol Byler Annie came into the shop with snacks to pass around for the younger children: a plate of sugar cookies, graham crackers, and a pitcher of water with cups. This broke the monotony and was a pleasant diversion for them. Lakisha snacked. Nancy, however, decided she was too old for that.

Over on the boys' side, Andrew was sitting beside Junior Byler. Just after the second preacher stood up, Junior whispered to Andrew, "I'm going to get some sleep. Wake me up when it's time to kneel."

Andrew nodded, then whispered back, "I'll poke you good and hard."

However, mischief was brewing in Andrew's mind. Would he dare to play a trick on Junior, and poke him now, before it was time to kneel? The more he thought of it, the more he wanted to do it.

Junior was fast asleep, with his head leaning forward on his chest.

In his mind, Andrew shaped an excuse: *It would serve him right for sleeping in church.*

Then, suddenly, he reached out and jabbed Junior in the ribs. Quick as a flash, unsuspecting Junior turned, dropped to his knees, and knelt by the bench, not realizing he was the only one.

All was quiet for a few seconds, then Junior heard a snicker. He lifted his head, and suddenly the situation dawned on him. With his face flaming, he quickly got up again and sat down, sure that every eye in the shop was on him. Junior wished the floor would open up and swallow him.

Beside him, Andrew was having struggles of his own. Seized with a wild desire to laugh, he gulped and tried to keep his shoulders from shaking, but it was a losing battle. Since he was almost choking from holding laughter back, he quickly stood up, reached for his hat, and went outside.

Out in the barn, Andrew laughed wildly until he collapsed on a bale of hay. "Poor Junior!" he scoffed. "Didn't he ever look like a *Schnepp* (simpleton)! It serves him right, though."

Suddenly the barn door opened, and Deacon Miller walked in.

"Andrew," he asked sternly, "did you think it was right for you to play a trick like that on Junior Byler, especially during a worship service?"

Andrew hung his head. He had thought no one noticed what he did, but he should have known better. That thought sobered him up fast.

"*Ya* (yes), I should be ashamed of myself," he admitted lamely. "But Junior was sleeping on purpose. He told me he wanted to get some sleep . . . and . . . I . . ."

"Yes, Junior was in the wrong, too," Deacon Miller counseled quietly. "But two wrongs don't make a right. Come, Andy, let's go in now." The deacon put an arm around Andrew's shoulders for a few steps as they headed out of the barn.

Andrew meekly followed the deacon into the

shop and sat down beside Junior again. Now it was *his* turn to feel on the spot. He knew everyone was eyeing him, and his face burned with shame. Why did everyone keep staring at him so?

He heard a few choked-back giggles, which increased his discomfort. What was wrong?

Then Junior leaned over to whisper, "You forgot to take your hat off."

Poor Andrew! He thought he'd never been so utterly humiliated in his life, but he knew he deserved it. His prank had boomeranged, and he had fallen into the very pit of embarrassment that he had dug for Junior.

Next time I'll think twice before I play a trick on someone else, he thought miserably. And then that Bible verse came to his mind: "Be sure your sin will find you out."

9

Fresh Air Boy

NANCY carefully guided the sopping wet clothes through the wringer on the washing machine and pulled them out on the other side. This was the first time she was doing the laundry all alone, and she wanted to make sure she did everything right. She hoped she wouldn't clog the wringer and stall the engine as she had once done at home.

Jacob came into the washhouse. Above the roar of the gas engine, he shouted, "I'm going to be working in the *Fruchtkammer* (granary). If you need me for anything, you can find me there."

Nancy nodded.

"Make sure you don't get your hand caught in the wringer," Jacob teased.

Nancy blushed. *As if I'm a glee Meedel (little girl)!* she thought indignantly.

Cooking the meals was another challenge for Nancy. At home there was always Mother's guiding hand and wise counsel. Here she was on her own. Mary was already hobbling around on crutches a little. But most of the time, her leg was still too painful for her to be up.

By late morning, the wash was on the line, flapping merrily in the breeze. Nancy scrubbed the concrete floor of the washhouse with a broom and a bucket of rinse water. Then she went into the kitchen, wondering what she could prepare for dinner.

Mary came hobbling out of the bedroom. "My, it's nice to have such a good *Maut* (helper)," she exclaimed. "I'm so glad you're here. Sally's mother just dropped in and brought a casserole and a dessert for our *Middaagesse* (noon meal).

"It sure is a blessing to have some of *unser Leit* (our people) for neighbors. And not just *unser Leit* are helping us. Mrs. Davis took us to the doctor. We are surrounded by a sea of kindness."

The casserole and dessert were delicious. Nancy was glad she didn't need to cook the meal.

To her surprise, the next day Sol Bylers brought in one meal. They informed Mary and Nancy that each day of that week, one of their Amish neighbors was scheduled to bring a meal. The women of the neighborhood planned this after church, where they heard the news of Mary's misfortune.

Mary and Jacob felt humbled and unworthy to be on the receiving end of such helpfulness. They resolved to do more to help others in time of need.

On Wednesday morning Sally and Lakisha came over. "I'm going home today," Lakisha shared sadly. "I wish I could stay all summer."

"We're inviting you back for next summer," Sally consoled her. "Then you can stay for *four* weeks."

"Great! I'd love that!" Lakisha's face was bright and eager.

"We're getting a little boy now for two weeks," Sally told Nancy. "I wonder what he'll be like."

"I'll bet Andrew's glad," Nancy commented.

"He sure is. He keeps saying how henpecked he's been, as the only boy. We ought to make him promise not to tease the Fresh Air boy, though."

"I hope he likes staying with you as much as I did," Lakisha put in. "I can't wait for next summer."

"Same here," Sally agreed. "But we've got to go now."

"Good-bye, Lakisha." Nancy shook hands with her. "I hope I get to see you next summer."

"So do I!" Lakisha exclaimed warmly. "From now on, I'm coming back every year!"

That evening Sally and Andrew came over with the new Fresh Air boy. His name was Tyler Alexander, and he had curly black hair, a wide smile with two front teeth missing, and the darkest skin that Nancy had ever seen. He said he was ten years old.

"Do you want to see the horses?" Andrew asked. "Jacob has six workhorses and a carriage horse."

"The horses are in the meadow right now," Nancy told him. "You can climb up on the fence to watch them."

"Do you really live so close to a park?" Tyler wondered in amazement. "You could go to the park every day! All this green grass!" He swept his arms around in a big arc.

"And the sky is so blue and seems so close. At home I have to stay near our front steps all summer long. It's too dangerous to go further, and there's not much to do. Can we go fishing in this park?"

"This isn't a park; it's a meadow," Nancy told him. "But Jacob won't mind if you'd like to go fishing. We'll ask him if you can use his fishing rod."

Poor boy, she thought, *sitting by the front steps on a hot street all summer! No wonder city children get in with gangs later!*

"I want to see the cows now," Tyler said. "How do they give milk?"

Nancy opened the door to the dairy barn, and they filed inside. For a few moments Tyler stood fascinated by the rows of feeding cows. Then he darted over to the nearest cow, knelt by her side, reached for her udder, and began to pull on her teat.

Whack! The cow lifted a hind foot and kicked, just missing Tyler's leg. Tyler jumped back, lost his balance, and fell over backward under the next cow in the stall.

"Tyler! Tyler!" Nancy and Sally both gasped as they sprang into action. Andrew calmed the cow while the girls pulled Tyler out from underneath, helped him up, and brushed the dirt off him.

"Don't you ever do that again!" Andrew scolded. "You have to be gentle with cows. Besides, you don't ever approach a cow without talking to her first, so she knows you're there and won't be scared.

"And never milk a cow from the left side—always from the right. These cows aren't used to being milked by hand either. Milking machines do the job here."

Tyler stood there blinking in confusion. "But I'd like to see the milk come out," he pouted. "That's why I wanted to come."

"Well, all right, I'll show you," Andrew agreed. "You stay there on the other side of the gutter, and I'll milk a few squirts."

"Whoa, Bossy," Andrew said to the cow as he patted her and knelt on her right side.

Tyler obediently squatted down on the other side of the gutter to watch.

"Open your mouth," Andrew instructed.

Tyler opened his mouth as though for a big yawn, and Andrew neatly directed a few squirts of milk into it.

"Aaghh!" Tyler sputtered. "This milk's warm." He backed away, licking a few drops from his face.

Nancy and Sally couldn't help but laugh.

"Of course it is," Andrew responded. "Come, and I'll show you the tank where it gets cooled."

"I want to taste this brown cow's milk first." Tyler had a gleam of mischief in his eye.

The brown cow was a jersey that Jacob kept with his herd of holsteins to raise the butterfat content in the tank of milk.

"All right, I'll give you a taste," Andrew agreed, kneeling down by the jersey. "Squat close, but stay on the other side of the gutter."

Tyler, pretending innocence, squatted down and picked up a friendly barn kitten that was nearby.

"Open your mouth," Andy instructed, aiming the squirt of milk toward Tyler's mouth.

Instead, quick as a flash, Tyler tossed the kitten on the jersey's back and stood back to see what would happen. The kitten dug its claws in and clung frantically to the cow's back.

The cow hunched her back, bellowed with pain, and kicked. Whack! Andrew flew over sideways and landed in the gutter!

"Oh, I'm sorry, awfully sorry." Tyler suddenly seemed all politeness and concern. He grabbed Andrew's hand and tried to help him up. "Are you hurt?" he asked, with wide-eyed innocence.

Andrew got up and tried to brush off the wet manure and dirt. "You rascal!" he cried, grabbing Tyler by the front of the shirt. "You'd better not try something like that again!"

Tyler only giggled helplessly.

As soon as Sally saw that Andrew wasn't hurt, she began to laugh wildly. "At last Andrew has found his match," she crowed, between spasms of laughter. "I thought I'd never see the day. That was a sight for sore eyes!"

Andrew glared at her, then he began to laugh, too. "This little guy isn't as dumb as he looks," he admitted, with a hint of respect in his voice. "I could use a brother like him."

"He's smart, all right." Sally was still laughing. "I sure hope he gives you plenty of your own medicine while he's here. I sure hope so."

10

The Pigeon Hunt

THE week passed quickly, and Friday evening arrived. Sally came into the milk house for milk while Nancy was still scrubbing the milkers.

"Hurry up and finish that job," she urged Nancy. "Andrew is ready to head for Aquila Riehl's barn soon. We want to play *Blummesack* (bag tag) awhile, too, before the pigeons roost. Junior and Barbie Byler are going along, too."

"Ya well, I'll hurry. It sounds like fun. Is Tyler going along?"

"Nope, definitely not. He'd be sure to fall down a hay hole. He sure is a live wire."

Twilight was already settling over the countryside as Nancy skipped over to the Fishers fifteen minutes later. A bat darted close to Nancy and disappeared. Night insects were calling, and the cows were mooing softly in the meadow as they headed down the cow lane to graze.

Junior and Barbie were already at the Fishers' place when Nancy got there. Junior had forgiven Andrew for the prank he played on him during the church service, and they were best of friends again.

The boys carried bright flashlights and empty feed sacks. Sally toted the *Blummesack,* which was a few rolled up flower-print sacks, tied together in the middle with baler twine.

The game of *Blummesack* was played like ball tag, except that one threw the *Blummesack* instead of a ball. Since it was soft, it wouldn't hurt anyone. The barn had plenty of hiding places, too, to keep from getting tagged so easily.

"It's a good thing I got permission from Aquila Riehl last week to catch pigeons in his barn," Andrew remarked. "I saw him going away just a little while ago in his trottin' buggy."

"Probably going to see his girl to ask her to marry him," Junior said.

"Huh!" Sally scoffed. "He did that long ago already. He's getting married in November, they say."

For Nancy's benefit, she continued, "This summer he's with the class of applicants for baptism and joining church. His sister Rachel was keeping house for him, but she had to go home and help her mother for a few weeks this summer. So now he has to batch it alone until she comes back."

The half-mile walk to Aquila's farm was covered

quickly, and there was time for a rousing game of *Blummesack* before it was too dark to see. Junior was *it* first. He closed his eyes and counted to fifty while the rest scrambled for hiding places.

Nancy hid behind the grain binder first, then sneaked over behind the *Fruchtkammer* (granary) door. As her eyes became accustomed to the semi-darkness, she noticed a white object on the ledge above her head. She reached up and took it down.

By the light of the granary window, she saw that it was a pack of chewing tobacco. Feeling guilty for snooping, she quickly replaced the pack. It was none of her business, she decided, as to why it was there and who had put it there. She would just pretend that she hadn't seen it.

Judging by the rollicking laughter and the sounds of running and dodging, she knew the others were being found. A moment later the granary door was flung forward, and the *Blummesack* came flying, hitting Nancy on the shoulder.

She grabbed the *Blummesack* and dashed after the one who had thrown it. Someone dodged behind a stack of bales. Nancy sneaked the other way around and threw the *Blummesack.* There was Andrew, looking back over his shoulder and expecting her to come that way, when wham! the *Blummesack* hit him squarely in the face!

"Okay, you *Schnickelfritz* (mischievous child), whoever you are, I'll get you back," he growled.

Nancy was giggling helplessly, but she managed to duck quickly and crawl under the corn planter. Maybe he wouldn't see her there. She sure had settled a few scores with him by now.

"All right, you *Meed un Buwe* (girls and boys), it's time to stop," Junior called just then. "We have to be quiet and let the pigeons roost. Let's sit here on these bales and tell ghost stories."

One by one the others came out of their hiding places. Nancy was trying hard to stop giggling, and Andrew was still grumbling to himself.

"Tell the story about eeeck, eeeck, give me my liver back," Barbie begged Sally. "You're the best storyteller."

"All right, be quiet and I will," Sally said importantly. All settled down on hay bales to listen. Sally *was* a superb storyteller. Her spine-tingling ghost stories made the shivers and chills run up and down their backs.

"Listen!" cried Junior, holding up his hand for silence. "The pigeons are coming."

There was a soft whirring of wings, and then a contented cooing as the pigeons settled on high barn-frame beams for the night.

"Bring the flashlights," Andrew whispered. "Let's go."

The girls held the flashlights, which would blind the pigeons long enough for them to be caught. The boys climbed up with the sacks. Some pigeons escaped and flew away, but the boys managed to grab six on their first try and stuffed them into the sacks. Later they got three more.

"This is a good catch," Andrew declared. "I'll send these to the Friday market, and we can divide the *Geld* (money)."

"*Was is sell* (what's that)?" Barbie asked suddenly. "Do I hear music?"

Sure enough! It sounded faint and far away, but it definitely was music.

"Let's follow the sound," Junior said eagerly, "and see where it's coming from."

"Be quiet!" he scolded Barbie, who had tripped over something. "We've got to sneak, or we'll never find out."

They all stepped silently out through the little door to the barn hill. Clouds scudded in front of the moon, and Nancy shuddered. What if there was an *Englischer* (non-Amish) hiding somewhere nearby?

"Follow along," Andrew whispered.

They skirted the silo and went down around to the back of the barn, where the tobacco-stripping room was. There the music was louder and plainer.

"There's a light in the stripping room," Nancy noticed. "Let's peep inside."

They squatted down in the bushes near the windows.

"It's Aquila," Sally whispered. "He has—"

"Shhh!" Andrew ordered. "We can see for ourselves."

By the light of the lantern on the table inside, they could see that Aquila was looking at a newspaper, and on the table beside him was a radio, blaring away.

"Come! Let's go before he sees us," Barbie whispered.

They quickly ran around to the other side of the barn.

"There's Aquila's rig." Junior was waving at the buggy by the barn. "I didn't hear him come home."

"I'm going to tell Dad that Aquila has a radio," Andrew vowed stoutly. "He ought to know better. Dad can tell Deacon Miller. Aquila won't get away with that, if he's going to be a member of the church!"

"Would you really?" Barbie asked. "What if Aquila finds out that you tattled?"

"*Ich geb nix drum* (I don't care)," Andrew declared stubbornly. "He's *grosshunsich* (uppity)."

"Ach, Andrew, he's no worse than you yourself are for *grossfiehlich* (feeling important)," Sally scolded. "Did you like it when Deacon Miller went out to the barn to talk to you?"

"*Ich geb nix drum*," Andrew repeated. "I think it would be best to tell."

"All right, go ahead," Junior agreed. "I don't think Aquila knew we were there at all. He wouldn't know who reported him."

They walked home together, carrying the pigeons in the sacks. Nancy felt troubled by their discovery and also about the chewing tobacco she had found on the barn ledge.

If Aquila was joining the church, why did he have these things? Raising tobacco was traditional, a way to make a living on fewer acres. But chewing it was a bad habit, to be discouraged.

Mary and Jacob were waiting up for Nancy when she walked into the kitchen. "Well, did you catch any pigeons?" Jacob asked. "Or was it like trying to catch *Elbedritschlin* (snipes, imaginary animals)?"

"No, we caught nine," Nancy replied. "But what kind of a boy is Aquila? Sally said he's joining church, but he had a radio."

Nancy told them what they had seen in the stripping shed.

"I'm surprised at Aquila," Mary commented sadly. "It doesn't sound like he's sincere. What's the point of joining church if behind their backs he has things that are *verboten in die Ordnung* (against the church rules)?

"He's going with Laura Kaufman, and she's a nice girl. Maybe she'll help him to do better and to be an upbuilding church member."

"Ya, maybe that's what Aquila needs," Jacob agreed. "Some say the church rules are just man-made, but they're all for a good reason. Plain and common, without worldly excess—that's best."

He got up and stretched himself so that his fingers touched the ceiling. "Time for bed," he announced. "The cock will be crowing before we're ready for it."

Later, Nancy lay in bed, thinking over the evening. Through the screened window she heard the tree frogs chirping and the katydids calling, just like they did at home. She was engulfed by a wave of *Heemweh* for Whispering Brook Farm.

Nancy wondered if tonight Mom had told Susie and Lydia their bedtime stories as usual. Had Joe washed his buggy for the weekend? Had Omar curry-combed his horse, Beauty? Had Steven and Henry played out in the orchard until it was too dark to see?

Maybe *Maami* (Grandma) had come over from

the *Dawdy* (grandparents') end of the house and visited awhile. Dad had likely read aloud out of the Bible.

Nancy thought of *Daadi* (Grandpa), who was no longer with them, and her eyes filled with tears. No, she simply would not allow herself to yield to *Heemweh*. Now she was needed as Mary's *Maut* (helper), not just on a vacation, and she would be brave.

"*Der Herr ist mein Hirte, mir wird nichts mangeln* (the Lord is my shepherd, I shall not want)," she murmured. With that, she drifted off into a peaceful sleep.

11

Angry Hornets

IT was Sunday morning. No work today, except the usual chores. Nancy stretched luxuriously in bed. There was no hurry this morning because it was the in-between Sunday, with no church.

Because of Mary's injured leg, they weren't going visiting either. Probably some folks would stop by in the afternoon to see how Mary's leg was coming along.

Nancy turned over and relaxed, reveling in the lovely early-morning sounds coming through the screened window: a banty rooster crowing in the barnyard, a turtledove cooing from the old spruce, a robin cheerily singing from the maple tree, a cardinal whistling from a tree in the meadow, a calf bawling for its breakfast, and then the sound of Jacob starting up the diesel to begin milking.

Nancy sprang out of bed. It was too lovely a day to lie abed. Now Jacob was singing the *Lobleid* (Praise song), and the rich melodious tunes were floating in through the window on the fragrant morning breeze.

Nancy hurried with her chores. She wanted to surprise Mary and Jacob by making waffles for breakfast as a special treat. Nancy knew Mary had a waffle iron, for she had seen it in the cellar way.

I want to be careful now, and not burn them like I did the Knepplin, Nancy thought, as she washed the calf buckets. *Mary mentioned once that Jacob is fond of waffles, and I want them to be just right.*

In the kitchen, Mary sat on the rocker, watching Nancy mixing the batter.

"Oh Nancy," she exclaimed. "Words cannot express how *dankbaar* (thankful) I am that you're here and are such a good helper! We simply couldn't manage without you. Jacob and I were just talking about it last night, wondering what we could get you for a gift. What would you like to have?"

Nancy's eyes twinkled. "Well, one thing I'd like to have is a little niece or nephew," she said impishly.

"Ach my," Mary chuckled. "You sure don't ask for much, do you?"

"Well, there are a lot of things I'd like to have. But that would be the nicest gift I could think of."

Nancy put a clean white tablecloth on the table, and in the center she placed a bouquet of freshly cut gladioli. It made the table look so pretty. Then she hurried to finish making the waffles.

Beginner's luck was with Nancy. The waffles turned out crisp and light, delicious and golden-browned to perfection.

"*Wunderbaar gute* (wonderfully good)," Jacob pronounced them at the breakfast table, as he poured maple syrup over them. "Lucky the man that gets you for a cook, Nancy. Already you're almost as good a cook as Mary is."

Nancy blushed at the praise. "I'm getting a lot of experience here," she said. "Sometimes I'm afraid I'm treating you like guinea pigs with my experimenting. It's a wonder you survive, eating some of my flops."

"Now Nancy, don't throw away Jacob's compliment," Mary chided gently. "You're doing a good job."

The door opened, and in walked Sally, Andrew, and Tyler.

"Still eating breakfast?" Andrew quipped.

"Yes, and for a good reason, too," Jacob told him. "Come and taste a bite of Nancy's good waffles."

"We'd better not," Andrew replied. "We're planning a picnic for dinner, and we'd better save some room for that."

Sally spoke up, "We had a picnic for Lakisha. Now we want to have one for Tyler, too, since he has to go home in a few days. May Nancy go with us?"

"Certainly. I'll do the dishes for you this time so you can go sooner," Jacob offered kindly. "But don't count on me washing them every day! I have to keep the farm going, you know."

"Thanks, Jacob," Nancy responded.

In a short time, the youngsters were happily tramping through the meadow. Andrew was carrying a jug of tea, and the girls were carrying the picnic basket between them.

"I'll set the tea in the spring to keep it cool until lunchtime," Andrew planned.

Tyler ran happily about, gathering twigs and firewood.

"Look what I found!" Nancy cried happily, bending over to retrieve something from the grass. "A four-leaf clover!"

Sally was envious. "That's supposed to mean you'll have good luck. I hope I find one, too. Say, what's that on your hand, Nancy? I never noticed it before."

"Just a few warts. I've had them for as long as I can remember."

"Do you want to know how to get rid of them?" Andrew asked.

Without waiting for a reply he went on. "You take a turnip, go out under the full moon, cut the turnip in two, rub your warts with one half, and say, 'One two three, Warts away from me.'

"Then rub them with the other half and say, 'One two three four, Warts vex me no more.' Finally, bury the turnip. Soon you won't have the warts anymore."

"Ach, Andrew, that's just gibberish," Sally scolded. "Next Nancy will believe you. I can tell you a real remedy, Nancy. Just pick a milkweed pod, break it open, and spread the milky center over the warts. It really works. I tried it on mine, and they disappeared."

"Hey, what's that big thing way up high in the tree?" Tyler asked. "I'd like to knock it down."

"Whoa there! You'd better not try that," Andrew warned. "That's a hornets' nest. If one of them stings you, you'll wish you hadn't meddled with them. They can get real angry."

"But I want to see a live hornet," Tyler protested. "If it would try to sting me, I'd slap it dead."

"You'd find out how fast a hornet can sting," Sally told him. "But that looks to me like an old nest. Maybe the hornets have all moved away."

"Don't count on it," Andrew warned. "Just let the nest be, and the hornets will leave us be."

"Who comes there, walking along the creek?" Nancy asked. "It looks like two *rumschpringing* boys (Amish youth sixteen or older, running around)."

"You're right. They're Eli and Ben, Dan D.'s sons," Andrew said. "It looks like we're going to have help to eat our picnic lunch."

Eli and Ben walked over to the picnic basket. "What have we here?" Eli joked. "Sandwiches! Just what we need. Yum yum."

He started to unwrap one and pretended to take a bite.

"You leave that be!" Tyler shouted, running to Eli and pummeling him with his fists. "It doesn't belong to you!"

"Ho, what's this?" Eli exclaimed, in surprise. "A little black spitfire? Here, Ben, help me throw him in the creek. A good ducking is what he needs."

But Tyler was too quick for them. Quick as a flash, he darted away, picked up a stone, and aimed for the hornets' nest, right above the heads of Ben and Eli. Tyler hit his target, and suddenly an angry stream of hornets zoomed toward the offenders.

"*Hannesel! Hannesel! Schpring,* Eli! (hornets! Run)," Ben yelled.

Andrew grabbed Tyler's arm and held him still. "Don't run! Drop to the ground and hold still," he told the picnic party.

Eli and Ben were running and waving their arms over their heads. The angry hornets, attracted by the motions, followed them.

As soon as they were a distance away, Andrew said, "Now girls, get the tea and the basket and we'll hurry off."

He led Tyler, and they went on up the creek until they were safe.

"Whew! That was a close call," Andrew sighed in relief. "I wonder how Eli and Ben fared. They're probably covered with stings."

"It serves them right!" Tyler exclaimed. "They were going to steal our food."

"They were just pretending," Sally assured him. "But anyway, thanks to you, Tyler, we got rid of them fast. I just hope neither of them is allergic to hornet stings."

"And thanks to Andrew's quick thinking, none of us were stung," Nancy added admiringly. "I was ready to take off like a frightened rabbit."

Andrew chuckled, "I learned that lesson the hard

way a few years ago. The more you run and yell and wave your arms, the more you attract angry hornets."

"Hey, let's get busy and build our campfire," Tyler chattered eagerly. "Can we go fishing, too?"

"Nope, not today," Sally told him. "We don't go fishing on Sundays. We may fish on days like Good Friday, Ascension Day, and sometimes Saturdays or weekday evenings.

"Today we'll go hiking, and wading in the creek. And I have my binoculars along for bird watching."

"Let's build a dam across the creek with stones," Andrew suggested. "Then I'll whittle a boat for you, Tyler, and show you how to skip stones across the creek."

The day passed quickly and happily. On the way back from the picnic, they met Junior and Barbie coming down the road on scooters.

"Did you hear how Ben and Eli were stung by hornets?" Junior asked. "There must be a big hornets' nest somewhere around here."

"Were they?" Andrew pretended not to know anything about it. "How bad was it?"

"Bad enough that they can't go to the singing tonight. They didn't get sick, but they just don't want to be seen swollen up like that," Junior answered.

"What a relief!" Sally whispered to Nancy. "After all, it was Tyler's fault that the hornets came out, and Tyler is our responsibility."

Nancy nodded. "It could have been worse. But all's well that ends well."

12

Cleaning Girl

"MARY, there's a car in the lane, and a lady is coming to the door," Nancy told her sister on Monday. "Do you know her? She walks with a cane."

Mary came out of the bedroom on crutches. "Why, that's Mrs. Bailey, the neighbor from the big house on the hilltop. She probably came for the pound of homemade butter she ordered."

"Come in, Mrs. Bailey," Mary called. "I've got your butter wrapped and ready. Nancy can bring it up from the cellar."

"Oh, my goodness, what happened to you?" Mrs. Bailey gasped. "Did you break your leg?"

While Mary explained, Nancy went to get the butter, then sat listening to the conversation. Mrs. Bailey looked like a keen old lady. Her face was framed with curly white hair, and her eyes were blue. "It looks like you have a good helper with your sister here," Mrs. Bailey said, turning to Nancy.

"I sure do," Mary agreed. "She works so fast that I can hardly keep her busy."

Mrs. Bailey laughed. "Well, well, if that's the case, maybe I could borrow her for a few hours each week. I have so many antiques and knickknacks to dust in my house, and I can't be on my feet too much. A young Amish girl to help me is just what I need.

"Would you like to work for me, Nancy? I'd gladly pay you five dollars an hour."

Nancy's eyes widened. *Five dollars an hour!* At home she would have to pick many boxes of strawberries to earn five dollars. She looked at Mary. "Do you think I could?"

"Let me talk it over with Jacob first," Mary replied. Then she added to Mrs. Bailey, "You know, don't you, that Nancy's going home when school starts?"

"Yes, I figured as much." Mrs. Bailey nodded. "I'm hoping my feet will be better by then so I can get caught up with my work. If Nancy is allowed to come and help me, I'll stop by for her on Wednesday morning at nine o'clock."

Thus Wednesday morning found Nancy in Mrs. Bailey's car, headed for her new job. She was feeling butterflies in her stomach again, but she supposed that five dollars an hour was worth it.

Mrs. Bailey was friendly and talkative, and Nancy

soon felt at ease with her. "We moved into this area a little over a year ago," she told Nancy. "There are a lot of things I'd like to ask about you Amish people, if you don't mind."

"Oh, I don't mind," Nancy assured her. "But maybe I won't be able to answer everything you want to know. You could ask my sister Mary. She could tell you more."

"Maybe I will. Well, here we are at my house." Mrs. Bailey drove up the long winding drive, right into the garage. As soon as they were inside, the garaged door closed all by itself.

Nancy was astonished. *Another one of the englisch inventions*, she thought. The house amazed Nancy, too. Such tall windows, from the floor to the peak of the roof! A wide, curving stairway led up to a large open balcony.

Soft deep carpeting covered the floors everywhere. Nancy saw soft luxurious recliners, floor-length drapes, sparkling chandeliers, and beautiful furnishings. In the kitchen she found an automatic dishwasher, a microwave oven, and other gleaming electric appliances.

Best of all was the air-conditioning throughout the house. Every room was cool and comfortable! Nancy felt like she was in the lap of luxury!

In the family room, Mr. Bailey sat in a recliner watching television. "Hello," he greeted her pleasantly. "So you're the girl who's going to do our dirty work! Welcome, and thanks for helping us out."

Then he went back to watching a baseball game on TV, blind to his surroundings.

Dirty work! Nancy thought. *I sure don't see any dirt around here. Maybe he calls dusting dirty work.*

Mrs. Bailey came with a soft cloth and a can of furniture polish. "I'll show you around and tell you what I want you to do. Then if you have any questions, just feel free to ask them."

First they went up the winding stairway to the balcony room. In it were shelves and shelves of books and numerous trophies.

"The books in this bookcase you never have to dust," Mrs. Bailey said, motioning to a tall bookcase with glass doors. "These are all very old and valuable. Mr. Bailey keeps it locked most of the time."

On the desk were more trophies, and everything had to be dusted. "Mr. Bailey was a ballplayer, and a good one too, when he was in high school and college," Mrs. Bailey exclaimed, with a hint of pride in her voice.

"That's one of the things I wanted to ask you about. I understand you people don't go to high school or college. Can you tell me why not?" She sounded genuinely puzzled.

Nancy thought fast. "Well, I—I guess it's not really necessary for our way of living. Mostly we do things like farming and carpentry and shop work, and housekeeping."

"But couldn't an education be used to serve God, too? The Lord gave us minds, and shouldn't we do all we can to make the best use of the gifts and talents we received from God?"

"I—I don't know," Nancy replied. This was too deep for her. "I guess it's best to do things the way our parents taught us. There might be too many worldly temptations at high school and college."

"I'm not trying to condemn you," Mrs. Bailey hastened to add. "I was just wondering about some of your beliefs. Do you have Sunday school at church, or Wednesday evening Bible study?"

"No, we don't. Our parents teach us at home, and we read the Bible at home."

The telephone rang, and she was glad when Mrs. Bailey went to answer it. Nancy carefully dusted each object on Mr. Bailey's big desk. So many trophies! He must have been a real hero. Then she dusted the shelves lined with books and more trophies.

Nancy lifted the lid of a green ceramic turtle, and inside lay a key. *It wonders me if that's the key to the bookcase,* Nancy mused. *I'd like to see those old books, but I'd never dare to ask.*

Mrs. Bailey came back with a watering can. "I'll water the large basket planters hanging under the ceiling lights," she told Nancy. "When this room is finished, we'll go to the master bedroom."

While they worked together, Mrs. Bailey asked many more questions. From the bedroom closet, she pulled out a dark-blue pullover sweater. "This sweater is too small for me," she told Nancy. "Do you think you'd be able to wear it?"

"I—I guess not," Nancy said hesitantly.

"Oh, but why not? It's dark colored like your clothes are."

"Yes, it is, but we don't wear pullovers. We wear capes and aprons and shawls."

"I see. But do you all have to dress alike? Can you tell me why?"

My, she was curious! Nancy wondered how she could explain. "I—I guess so no one dresses for pride or for fancy," she explained. "We sew all our own clothes, and the simple patterns are easiest to make. We don't follow the fashions of the world."

That seemed to satisfy Mrs. Bailey. She got her car keys. "Mr. Bailey and I are going out to get some burgers and fries for lunch. You can do the dusting in the family room until we get back. We'll leave the TV on for you, so you can watch while you work."

Nancy knew that she should speak up and say she didn't want to watch television, but she felt timid.

"Oh well, I just won't watch it," she told herself. "I won't even look at it once. Not once!"

13

The Broken Dish

HOWEVER, Nancy's eyes were drawn to the TV screen like a magnet. On it a young man and woman were skating together. The man was fully dressed, but the woman's long legs were bare up to a short, ruffled skirt.

Never before had Nancy seen such graceful, beautiful, rhythmic skating. It was a flawless performance. In and out and around each other they skated. Sometimes it seemed as though their legs were intertwined, but they always disentangled again.

Nancy continued her dusting as she watched spellbound. Now the woman was twirling around fast in a circle on the tip of her skate. Nancy gasped as the man lifted the woman up high. It seemed as if she was falling headfirst onto the ice, but at the last moment she landed on her skates with marvelous agility and was skating with him again.

Crash! Nancy's mind was jolted back to her work by tinkling glass. With dismay she viewed the broken dish on the floor. It had slipped out of her hands and hit the corner of the coffee table, breaking into three big pieces.

"Oh no! What have I done now?" she moaned. "A broken *Schissel!* Why didn't I watch what I was doing?"

She quickly picked up the shards of the green candy dish from the floor, wondering what she could do with them. Without thinking of the consequences, she grabbed a small shovel by the fireplace and carried the glass out the back door.

Behind a row of spruce trees, she found some soft dirt and quickly buried the glass, just like she had buried the *Knepplin.*

"There now, no one will find out," she consoled herself. "Mary has a dish that looks almost exactly like the one that broke. I'm sure she'll let me have it, and next week I'll bring it along. The Baileys probably won't even notice that it's gone and won't know the difference."

If Nancy thought that would make her feel better, she was mistaken. Quickly she cleaned the shovel and put it back in place. She felt miserable, knowing that she ought to confess.

Now she had no problem keeping her eyes averted from the TV set. She tried to hurry with the dusting and yet be careful not to break anything else.

A few minutes later the door opened and the Baileys walked in. "Back again," Mrs. Bailey called. "I'll have our lunch ready in a jiffy."

A short while later, she called Nancy to the kitchen. "I hope you like hamburgers, fries, and milkshakes." She smiled. "It's the typical American fast food."

Nancy nodded and sat on a stool at the counter with the Bailey couple. She didn't feel hungry since she was so absorbed in feeling guilty about the dish she had broken.

Mrs. Bailey took a bite of her hamburger. "Is something wrong, dear?" she asked Nancy. "Why aren't you eating?"

Nancy was used to praying before eating, but she decided not to bow her head in front of the Baileys. She took a sip of her milkshake. "This is good," she said politely.

"Well, did you watch TV?" Mr. Bailey asked, his eyes twinkling.

Nancy nodded and suddenly felt ashamed. Maybe they had only wanted to test her, and she had failed the test. If she hadn't watched TV, she wouldn't have carelessly broken the dish.

Mr. Bailey chuckled. "Don't feel bad about it. Everyone's just human." But it was obvious that he was greatly amused.

Nancy guessed that he was making fun of her. Her face burned with shame. She wondered what the Baileys would say if they knew about the broken dish.

After lunch Mrs. Bailey announced, "I'd like you

to help me wash some windows now. Then in an hour or so, I'll take you home. You're a good worker, and I'm quite pleased with what you've done."

"Thank you," Nancy murmured.

But she felt unhappy inside. *Now is the time to confess about the dish,* her conscience told her. But Nancy couldn't bring herself to do it.

After the windows were finished, Mrs. Bailey handed a small wrapped box to Nancy. "Here's a small gift for you." She smiled indulgently. "I want you to open it before you leave."

Nancy opened the box, and inside lay a wristwatch with a gold band. Nancy caught her breath. "I'm sorry," she said sadly. "We're not allowed to wear wristwatches."

For a moment Mrs. Bailey looked hurt. Then she suggested brightly, "Oh, but can't you wear the wristwatch under your sleeve, so no one will see it?"

Nancy shook her head. "That simply wouldn't do. Somebody would see it when I stretch my arm."

"But don't your menfolks have watches in their pockets?" Mrs. Bailey persisted. "You could keep the watch in your pocket, too, couldn't you? That wouldn't be the same as wearing it."

Nancy felt herself wavering. "That might be all right. Yes, maybe I'll do that. Thanks a lot, Mrs. Bailey." She tried to sound glad.

In the car on the way home, Nancy resolved, *I'm not ever going back. I'll get Sally to work there instead of me.* Her conscience was troubled, and she was worried about the dish. Now she had a wristwatch in her pocket, too.

Mrs. Bailey drove in the lane at Mary and Jacob's house and stopped. "I'll be here for you next Wednesday at nine o'clock," she promised. "And, oh, I almost forgot to give you your pay!"

She took two ten-dollar bills out of her purse and handed them to Nancy.

Twenty dollars for just doing a bit of cleaning! Nancy thought. Maybe it was worth it after all. It was more than she had ever had before.

"Thank you, Mrs. Bailey!" she said, her eyes shining. With a wave of her hand, she ran into the house.

Not till later did Nancy realize that she hadn't told Mrs. Bailey that this was her last time.

"Oh well, maybe next time it will go a lot better," she told herself. "Then I'll tell her that she has to get another cleaning girl."

14

A Farm Sale

THE next forenoon Nancy watched for her chance. When no one was watching, she slipped upstairs to her room and got the wristwatch. Out in the barn, she stood on the feed cart and hid it on a beam above the feedway.

The idea for a hiding place had come from Aquila's chewing tobacco. But she pushed the wristwatch far enough back so no one would be able to see it. "*Niemand fint es datt* (no one will find it there)," she muttered.

Quickly Nancy darted back to the house and carried on with her work. A few minutes later she heard a noise outside.

"Someone's whistling for you, Nancy," Mary

called from the bedroom.

Nancy put down the pan of lima beans she was shelling and went to the door. There was Sally, with her pony and cart, motioning for Nancy.

"*Kumm du raus* (come outside)," she called. "Don't you want to go along to the sale?"

"What sale?"

"At the old Smith place. Most of our friends are going. The boys will be playing *Eckball* (corner ball), and the girls will be jumping rope. Can you come?"

Jacob was heading for the house and overheard Sally. "I'm going too," he said. "Nancy, you may ride with me if Mary can spare you."

Nancy dashed into the house to check with Mary, who agreed. "Sure, you may go. Shelling lima beans is something I can do even though I'm on crutches."

Ten minutes later they were ready to go. Sally's pony had trotted on ahead, pulling her on the cart.

"Keep an eye on the old-fashioned secretary desk mentioned on the sale bill," Mary told Jacob. "I'd sure like to have it, if it doesn't go sky high. The *Sitzschtupp* (sitting room) needs another piece of furniture."

Jacob smiled at his wife indulgently. "If you want it, you shall have it. You deserve something for having to stay at home."

"Well, I'm sorry I can't go along," she sighed. "But don't pay more for the desk than it's worth."

As Nancy and Jacob neared the sale, they saw buggies, carriages, and spring wagons coming from all directions. Because of the other horses, King was excited and pranced even more than usual.

"Is it a farm sale?" Nancy asked. "I didn't expect to see so many of *unser Leit* (our people)."

"I guess you could call it that," Jacob replied, "although there are just a few acres. Old Mr. Smith had Clydesdale horses as a hobby, and lots of horse-drawn implements and shop tools. That's why so many Amish people are coming.

"Mr. Smith died not long ago, and now his things are being sold." Jacob tied the horse and then dug into his pocket. "Here's some money for you to buy something to eat."

Nancy hopped off the wagon and smiled. "*Danki* (thanks)."

The auctioneer was calling for bids. Over in a tent set up for the purpose, a women's group was selling chicken corn soup, subs, hamburgers, chips, candy bars, slices of cherry and shoofly pie, coffee, and soft drinks.

Across the yard, Nancy could see that a group of *Meed* were jumping rope on the *Scheierdenn* (barn floor).

"Oh, there's Sally," Nancy cried happily, and ran over to her friend.

"Let's go watch the *Eckball* game first," Sally proposed. "Andrew came earlier with Dad. I'd like to see him get put into the *Mosch* (mush, middle) and have to dodge the ball."

Nancy and Sally made their way through the crowd to the barn. There in the barnyard the boys had started a fast-paced game of corner ball.

"Let's climb the fence so we have a good view of the *Buwe* (boys)," Nancy suggested. "We'll be able to see everything from there."

"There's Andrew, in the *Mosch* already," Sally scoffed. "He'll probably have to stay there a long time."

Whiz! went the ball, flying from one boy to the next on the corners. Each catch scored a letter, *H, O, T—HOT*. If the ball was dropped, they had to start over.

But each time *HOT* was reached, they could aim for one of the boys in the *Mosch*. If he got hit, he had to stay in. But if he jumped or dodged successfully and was missed, the boy who threw the ball had to go into the *Mosch,* and the boy he missed took his place at the corner.

Nancy recognized many of the boys whom she had seen at church. How swiftly the ball flew from one boy to the next. When *HOT* was reached, the boy who caught the ball pretended to be throwing it to the one at the next corner, but at the last instant he aimed for Andrew.

However, Andrew was wary and ready for all the tricks. He threw himself flat on the ground, and the ball zoomed over him.

Secretly, Nancy was glad. Andrew had not teased her again, and he hadn't told anyone about the *Knepplin*. Inwardly, she was cheering for him.

But not Sally. "Humph!" she sniffed. "I've seen enough of *Eckball*. Let's go jump rope."

Although Nancy wanted to watch the corner ball game longer, she jumped off the fence with Sally, and they headed for the *Scheierdenn*. Two girls were swinging the long jump rope, and in the center, two girls were jumping.

Others were helping to chant in tune and in rhythm with each jump:

> Teddy bear, teddy bear, turn around.
> Teddy bear, teddy bear, touch the ground.
> Teddy bear, teddy bear, touch your shoe.
> Teddy bear, teddy bear, now skiddoo.

The girls who were jumping had to do just what was being said. On *skiddoo* they had to leap away from the rope without touching it.

Sally grabbed Nancy's hand. "Here we go!" she sang. Together they jumped into the action. The girls were now chanting,

> Cinderella, dressed in yellow,
> Went upstairs to kiss her fellow.
> By mistake she kissed a snake.
> [Nancy shuddered but kept skipping.]
> How many stitches did it take?
> One, two, three, four, five. . . .

Nancy was determined to last as long as Sally did, but at fifty-seven she tripped, and they both jumped out.

Several other girls hopped into the action as the girls started chanting,

> I went upstairs to make my bed.
> I made a mistake and bumped my head.
> I went downstairs to milk my cow.

I made a mistake and milked the sow.
I went in the kitchen to bake a pie.
I made a mistake and baked a fly.

Next one of the best jumpers hopped in and they started a rhyme to test her skill.

Mabel, Mabel, set the table,
Just as fast as you are able.
Don't forget the salt, sugar, vinegar,
mustard, red-hot *pepper!*

When they chanted *pepper*, the girls turned the rope faster and faster, until the jumper missed.

Then they used two long ropes rotating in opposite directions to skip double Dutch. Only the most nimble girls could last very long at that, as everyone chanted,

Sugar, salt, pepper, cider.
How many legs has a bow-legged spider?
One, two, three, four, five . . .

It was all such fun but tiring after a while.

"Let's go listen to the *Groier* (auctioneer)," Nancy gasped. "Jacob wants to buy the secretary desk, and I'd like to watch him bid."

They made their way across the yard to where the furniture had been set out. "Here it is." Nancy ran her hand across the slant front. It was old but solidly built of beautiful cherry wood. The girls opened all the doors and drawers and peeked inside.

"Look at this," Sally cried. "Here's a secret drawer, and it won't open. It must be locked."

"I just found a key taped under this little drawer!" exclaimed Nancy. "Let's unlock the secret drawer. Maybe it's full of valuable jewels."

She was about to take out the key when Sally alerted her that the *Groier* and crowd were coming their way. Quickly the girls closed the desk and stood back.

"Now how much am I bid for this beautiful secretary desk in mint condition?" the auctioneer called as the crowd milled around. "There's nary a scratch on it."

The bidding was lively at first, but as the price rose, bidding slowed. With a sigh of relief, Nancy saw that Jacob was the last bidder. She had been hoping so much that Mary would get her desk.

"Now we'll be able to look into the secret drawer," she whispered happily to Sally. "As soon as we get it home."

Sally nodded. "Wouldn't that be something if it was full of gold pieces or diamonds? I'm pretty sure it's something valuable, or the drawer wouldn't be locked. I can hardly wait to see what it is."

15

The Old Bible

THE auctioneer moved on and was selling off other items.

"Let's go and find something to eat," Sally said. "I'm hungry."

The girls made their way over to the huckster table, and each bought a sub and a soda. Then they watched the *Eckball* game until Nancy was satisfied, and spent the rest of the afternoon on the *Scheierdenn* with the other girls.

Nancy enjoyed the day and was sorry when she heard Jacob ask, "*Bisht du faddich fer geh* (are you ready to go)?"

The sale was over, so they went for their rig. Jacob drove King down the lane and tied him to the fence beside the yard. He went looking for a few men to help him load the desk onto the spring wagon.

"Hey!" Sally cried eagerly. "Let's go unlock that secret drawer now! I sure am eager to see if there's anything in it."

Quickly, before the men came, they got the key and unlocked the drawer.

"It's a book!" Sally was disgusted. "And here we were looking for valuable coins or jewels."

"It looks like an old Bible." Nancy carefully lifted it out of the drawer. She turned the pages and saw that it was indeed a Bible, and a German one, too.

Jacob came back with the men to load the desk. Nancy showed him the Bible and explained where she had gotten it.

Jacob looked the Bible over and hesitated. "I think I'd better show this to the auctioneer. It might be pretty valuable."

When Jacob returned, he told them, "Well, the auctioneer said that since the sale is over and there are no descendants of Mr. Smith's, the Bible belongs to us. We bought it with the desk. He doesn't know whether or not it's valuable.

"Now let's load the desk." They wrapped a blanket around the desk and then tied it fast with rope.

"We have a heavy load for King," Nancy remarked as they started off. "Do you think he'll be able to pull it?"

"If not, we'll hitch Sally's pony with him yet," Jacob teased.

Sally had driven up alongside them with her pony and cart. "Oh no, you won't!" she called. "I'll send Andrew and Dad over tonight to help unload the desk." Then she slapped the reins and her pony took off.

"King is a strong horse," Jacob assured Nancy. "He has no problem pulling this load."

"I can't wait to watch Mary's face when she sees the desk." Nancy hugged herself. "She'll sure be pleased."

Jacob nodded. "She deserves it. I really felt bad that I hadn't removed that stake from the garden, and she got hurt. But *so geht's* (so it goes). Too late we learn better."

As they turned in the lane at home, Nancy glanced toward the house. "There's Mary, sitting on the porch glider, waiting for us." She waved to Mary.

Jacob drove King across the yard and right up to the front steps. "A love offering for the queen of hearts!" he called jovially to Mary.

She smiled and blushed. "I hope you didn't have to spend a small fortune on it."

When they unwrapped it, Mary laughed with joy. "It's even nicer than I thought it would be."

"I think I may have gotten the desk for nearly nothing," Jacob told her. "There's an old Bible inside, and if I'm not mistaken, it's worth almost as much as I paid for the desk."

He got out the Bible and showed it to Mary. "See, it says here that it was printed in 1550, and that makes it over five hundred years old. It surely must be valuable. There are family records here in the front, and it's in really good condition. Somebody must have taken good care of it."

Just then Nancy noticed a familiar blue car coming in the lane, and her heart sank. What could the Baileys want now? Had they discovered that the green candy dish was broken? Why hadn't she confessed it right away?

Mary saw the car, too. "It's Mr. Bailey, coming for the pint of raspberries he ordered. Nancy, could you run and get it from the refrigerator?"

When Nancy came back, Mr. Bailey was admiring the secretary desk. "It's a fine piece," he was saying, "a real antique!"

Nancy sighed with relief. He wasn't saying anything about the broken dish.

"Here's something else I want you to look at." Jacob opened the desk, took out the big Bible, and handed it to Mr. Bailey.

Mr. Bailey's eyes lit up when he paged through the Bible. "This is a Froschauer Bible," he announced. "It's an original edition, printed in Zurich, Switzerland, and in surprisingly good condition.

"Hmmmm, let's see. Mr. Yoder, let me make you an offer. I'll give you a four-hundred-dollar check right now, for this Bible, if you're willing to sell it."

Jacob looked at Mary. "*Soll ich es verkaafe* (should I sell it)?" he asked. "Four hundred dollars is a lot of money."

Mary replied, " *'Sis uff zu dich* (it's up to you). Whatever you think."

"I don't think you'll get a better offer than that," Mr. Bailey assured them. "That's a good price."

Jacob studied the ground, then turned to Nancy. More jokingly than in earnest, he asked, "*Was soll ich duh* (what should I do)?"

Nancy shook her head. "*Ich wees net* (I don't know). But don't antiques and rare books become more valuable, the longer you keep them?"

"*Ya, sell is so* (yes, that's so)," Jacob replied.

By now he had made up his mind. "I guess we'll keep it," he told Mr. Bailey. "We never had an old Bible or any antique before."

Mr. Bailey threw his head back, clearly upset. "Let me tell you, I don't think you'll get another offer like this one. You're making a mistake."

His eyes narrowed. "You might not have another buyer for your Froschauer Bible if I can get one elsewhere."

"Well, thanks for the warning, but I guess we'll keep it," Jacob responded. He put the Bible back into the drawer.

Yet Mr. Bailey wasn't put off so easily. "Look here, Mr. Yoder," he persisted, "how much do you want for this Bible? State your price. I'll give you whatever you ask."

"No, I'm not selling it now," Jacob stated. "I've made up my mind."

Without another word, Mr. Bailey turned and headed for his car.

"He wasn't happy about it," Mary observed sadly. "Maybe we should have let him have it. Ach my, he forgot his raspberries. *Dabber* (quick), Nancy, run after him with them."

Nancy ran and caught up with him just after he

got into his car. He opened the car window. Without a word, he took the raspberries and handed out the money.

Then he muttered, "You tell Mr. Yoder that if he doesn't sell me that Bible, he'll wish he had. He surely will!" With that, he drove off.

At the supper table, Jacob commented, "Well, Nancy, thanks for saying what you did about antiques becoming more valuable. I just had it on the tip of my tongue to say Mr. Bailey could have it, but now I'm glad I didn't sell it. I wonder how much that Bible really is worth."

Nancy spoke up, "If you don't mind, I'd rather not clean for the Baileys anymore."

Suddenly she remembered the dish she wanted to replace, so she quickly added, "Unless Sally goes with me. Do you think she'd be allowed to?"

Mary promised to ask the Fishers if it would be all right, and Nancy felt as if it was a load off her shoulders. With Sally along, it would be more fun.

16

Dropping

ON Saturday morning Nancy was pushing the feed cart through the passage in front of the cows and giving each cow a shovelful. Andrew came strolling into the dairy barn, carrying his jug to be filled with milk.

"Do you want to help play *Blummesack* again this afternoon in Aquila Riehl's barn?" he asked. "Junior and Barbie are coming, and Sally and I will be there."

Nancy's eyes lit up. "Say, that would be fun!" she said enthusiastically. "We didn't have much time to play last Friday. Are you sure Aquila doesn't mind?"

"Ach nay," Andrew assured her. "I've helped him out a lot already, and I'm sure he doesn't care. His barn has the best hiding places, and it's halfway between here and the Bylers."

"All right. I'll be over after lunch," Nancy promised. "I usually get some free time then."

She quickly finished the feeding, then washed the cows' udders and began the teat dip. After that was finished, she got the big push brush and swept the walkways. Everything had to be spick-and-span to meet Jacob's standards and in case the milk inspector came.

"Why are you in such a big hurry?" Jacob wanted to know. "Did Andrew have something up his sleeve?"

"Just a *Blummesack* game," Nancy replied, "over in Aquila's barn this afternoon. Maybe if I hurry with my work, Mary can spare me."

Jacob grinned. "So that explains it. I figured as much. Well, be careful and look out for the hay holes."

When the milking was finished, Nancy quickly washed the milkers, took off her barn apron, and headed for the house. There was the Saturday work and cleaning to do, and some desserts to prepare for Sunday—maybe something easy like whipped Jello and cornstarch pudding.

When she reached the kitchen, Mary was sitting at the table mixing dough for half-moon pies. Nancy took the chance to ask for permission to go and play *Blummesack* that afternoon.

"Sure, you may go," Mary replied. "But be sure to be back by four o'clock. Company is coming for supper, and you won't want to miss that."

"Who is it?" Nancy wondered. "Someone I know?"

"It sure is." Mary's eyes were twinkling. "But Jacob and I decided to surprise you and not tell you who's coming! You'll just have to wait and see. They're bringing supper along, so it won't make extra work for us."

That news lent wings to Nancy's feet, and she sped about doing the cleaning, dusting, sweeping and mopping the floor, and shining the windows. The only people she could think of that might be coming were Sally and Andrew, and maybe Barbie and Junior, and perhaps some more of Sally's friends who had been at the mystery supper.

For dinner she made a quick, simple meal of lettuce-and-baloney sandwiches and home-canned vegetable soup. By one o'clock she was on her way to the Fishers.

Halfway there, Sally met her, leading the pony. She had been riding in a back field. "*Dummel dich!* (hurry up)," she called. "We've been waiting for fifteen minutes."

"I'm sorry," Nancy apologized, "but I had to help Mary bake the half-moon pies first. That's a hot job that takes a lot of time. I wish we could go for a swim first, in Bylers' pond."

"Well, we can't, not with the *Buwe,* anyway," Sally reminded her. "You know that on the days that the *Meed* are allowed to go swimming there, no *Buwe* are allowed, and vice versa. But today is girls' day, so maybe we could go tonight."

"I can't," Nancy told her. "We're getting surprise

visitors tonight. Do you know anything about it?"

"Nope." Sally shook her head. "It's probably a great-aunt or third cousin you hardly know anyway. Maybe you could slip away, and we could go swimming after all."

"I don't know, but I doubt it. Mary made it sound like it's someone special. I'll wait and see."

"C'mon, you slowpokes," Andrew called from the driveway. "*Ich kann net der ganz Daag waarde bis die Kieh heem kumme* (I can't wait all day till the cows come home)."

He grabbed Maggie's bridle from Sally, jumped on her back, dug his heels into her side, and galloped down the road toward Aquila's. "*Nau schpringet schtarick!* (now run fast)," he called back over his shoulder to the others.

"That Andrew," Sally grumbled, "he hasn't any *Geduld* (patience) whatsoever. I pity whoever gets him for a husband!"

"Well, maybe he'll grow up some more yet," Nancy suggested mildly. "He's not that bad."

"Hey!" Sally stopped suddenly, in the middle of the road. "You're not sticking up for Andrew, are you?"

"Of course not!" Nancy hastily responded. "He's your brother, and you know more about him than I do." She quickly changed the subject. "We have to *schpring schtarick* (run fast). Let's go!"

"Hmph!" Sally snorted. "I'm not going to run just because Andrew said so! It's too warm anyway. He needs to learn *Geduld.* I'm mad as a hornet at him, as you may already have noticed."

"*Fer was* (why)? What did he do?" Nancy wondered if Andrew really was as bad as Sally made him sound.

"We were having a pillow fight this morning, sneaking through the rooms after each other. I saw Andrew run into his room, so I stood at the doorway, out of sight, waiting to throw my pillow at him when he came out.

"Instead, he went out through another door, sneaked up behind me, and whammed me hard with his pillow, and over the head, too! It made me all *struwwlich* (messed-up hair), and he just roared with laughter. He was teasing me about it the rest of the forenoon."

Nancy tried hard to keep a straight face. She thought about how she had hit Andrew with the *Blummesack* when he was looking for her to come the other way. Did Andrew think Sally had hit him, or did he just want to get someone back for it, no matter who?

Aloud she said, "Why don't you just try to get him back when we're playing *Blummesack?* Then you can do the laughing."

Nancy thought about how the Fishers did not live on a farm and did not need to get up as early to do chores. She remembered what Dad used to say, "Idle time breeds mischief. Busy is best."

At Jacob's place, there was no time for a pillow fight before starting chores. But, of course, she knew that youngsters need time to play, too, such as *Blummesack* games. She would never forget that proverb, "All work and no play makes Jack a dull boy."

At Aquila's place, Junior, Barbie, and Andrew sat on the barn hill waiting for them. Andrew had tied the pony to a silo hoop. "Here come the slow-pokes," he greeted them with a grin. "Let's start!"

From the little barn door, Barbie tossed the *Blummesack* to Sally. "You're it first," she called. "Count to fifty."

The others quickly scrambled for hiding places. Nancy ran and ducked under the big flat wagon. Then, seeing that Andrew had the same plan, she crawled out on the other side and ran across the *Scheierdenn* (barn floor), heading for the feed grinder.

Sally was counting, "39, 40, 41, 42, 43. . . ."

Directly ahead of Nancy were a few hay bales, and she leapt over them. As she sailed through the air, she was horrified to see exactly where she would land—down a hay hole!

Nancy tried to keep herself from falling, but it was too late. The next instant she felt herself dropping through the air like a bomb toward the cement feedway floor below.

She tried to scream but could not make a sound. Dust flew around her. She squeezed her eyes shut, expecting the worst.

17

Eavesdropping

NANCY opened her eyes and blinked. At the last instant, she had grabbed at the sides of the hay hole, which had broken her fall, and she had landed on her feet. Besides, there was a mound of loose hay where she landed, which cushioned her fall. Weak with relief, Nancy walked away unhurt.

"*Bin ich immer dumm!* (am I ever dumb)," she muttered to herself. "It's bad enough when little children aren't careful to stay away from hay holes, and then fall down and break their heads. What would people think if they heard that a big girl like me was stupid enough to plunge down one? Ei yi yi!"

Suddenly Nancy stopped in her tracks. What was

that she heard? It sounded like men's voices, coming closer. What if they found her here, and she'd have to explain why?

She dashed through the feed alley and into the horse stable. Nancy yanked open the door to the harness closet, stepped inside, and pulled the door shut after her.

She heard a rolling door being pushed open, and then the voices were louder, coming nearer. She recognized one voice as Aquila's, since she had heard him in Jacob's dairy barn the other evening, when he had borrowed a welder.

But whose was the other voice? She knew she had heard it before, but where? It sounded like an older man. He seemed to be admonishing Aquila in a kindly but firm way.

"You have taken a step in the right direction," he was saying, "in making your application for church membership and baptism."

Suddenly Nancy knew who was speaking. It was Deacon Miller—she had heard him at church. Had he come to talk to Aquila about his radio?

He went on. "By making that step, you are giving a sign that you are willing to renounce the world, the flesh, and the devil, and to conform to the *Ordnung* (church rules).

"You know, of course, from your earliest memory, that radios are *verboten*. We do not feel that they benefit the Christian life. If we use our spare time listening to radio music and songs, how can we be spiritually minded and meditate on Bible verses and pray without ceasing?

"The Bible says, 'Let us lay aside every weight, and the sin which clings to us so closely.' Now, if you are sincere in expressing your desire for baptism, you will see your error and gladly put away all that is forbidden in the *Ordnung,* not so?"

"I *did* put away my radio," Aquila replied in a low voice. Nancy, hidden there in the harness closet, thought there was a hint of rebellion in his smooth voice.

"I sure am glad to hear that," Deacon Miller affirmed him heartily. "I have great hopes for you as a promising, steadfast church member. We expect you to be a good example to the younger generation, a light to the world, and the salt of the earth."

The deacon chatted a bit longer, about the weather and the price of cattle, and left before long. A few minutes later, Nancy heard the rattle of carriage wheels and the clop-clop of horses' hooves in the driveway and fading into the distance. Then all was quiet.

"So much for that," she heard Aquila mutter to himself. "It wasn't hard to get rid of him. I sure played a trick on him. When I said I put away my radio, he thought I meant that I had gotten rid of it. Well, this is how I put it away."

Nancy heard him opening a door. Soon the sound of radio music filled the air. It gave her a funny feeling. How could Aquila be so deceitful? Surely he knew better!

A moment later, Nancy choked back a scream. Something was twining itself around her ankles. Was it a snake? This time she screamed in earnest, too frightened to move.

Then she heard a soft purr. It was only a friendly cat, and its tail had curled around her ankles. "*Du alti Katz!* (you old cat)," she cried, weak with relief.

The harness closet door was jerked open, and there stood Aquila, staring open-mouthed at her.

"*Wu in die Welt kummst du her* (where in the world do you come from)?" he asked in amazement.

"I—I—," Nancy sputtered speechlessly. The radio was still blaring away, and without thinking she blurted out, "Why did you lie to Deacon Miller?"

The expression on Aquila's face changed from astonishment to anger. He grabbed the radio and threw it against the wall with such force that the crash of it shook the barn.

Aquila jumped up and down on the battered radio with both feet, all the while yelling at Nancy: "Mind your own business! Quit snooping! Get out of here! And keep your mouth shut."

Nancy had never before seen anyone so angry, and she was terribly frightened. Where could she run to? Quickly she dashed out of the horse stable, into the feed alley, looking for an outside door.

"Psst!" she heard someone say. Then again, "Psst, Nancy!"

She looked around but saw no one.

"Up here!"

Nancy looked up, and there were four faces looking down from the hay hole.

"Come up," Sally whispered, motioning with her hand. "See those stairs over there?" A moment later Nancy had joined her friends upstairs.

"We were listening from up here," Andrew explained in a low voice. "Boy, is he ever mad that he was found out! But it sure serves him right. Whew! Let's get out of here!"

Quietly they filed out through the little door to the barn hill.

"It's too bad our *Blummesack* game was spoiled," Sally grumbled. "But let's get ourselves away from here before Aquila sees us."

They hurried homeward, Junior and Barbie in one direction, Nancy and Sally the other way, with Andrew riding beside them on the pony.

"That sure beats all!" Andrew sputtered. "I wonder what Aquila will do now."

"Maybe it will help him to repent," Sally mused. "Or else he'll have to leave the class being instructed for church membership."

How sad! thought Nancy as she trudged homeward from the Fishers. *How can anyone be so blind, not foreseeing that his secret would surely come to light?*

She remembered what Moses said in the Bible, *Be sure your sin will find you out.*

18

Surprise Visitors

NANCY opened the screen door and stepped inside. Mary sat on the couch, smiling from ear to ear.

"*Was is so shpassich* (what's so funny)?" Nancy wondered. Then she heard a giggle from the other end of the kitchen and stopped in her tracks.

"Who's hiding behind the rocker?" she called. She tiptoed over and lifted the chair cover.

At that moment two small forms hurled themselves at Nancy, shouting, "Surprise! Surprise!"

"Susie and Lydia!" Nancy gasped. "Where do you come from? How did you get here?" She grabbed up two-year-old Lydia and held her close.

"We hid ourselves to scare you," Susie said, laughing gleefully.

As if that wasn't enough of a surprise, there came Mom out of the bedroom, smiling broadly. She walked over to Nancy and hugged her. "*Wie geht's* (how's it going), Nancy?" she asked, squeezing her hand. "Mary tells me that you've been doing a good job helping her, just like a much older girl would."

Nancy blushed at the unexpected praise. Being hugged and praised was something she was not used to, and she was surprised at Mom. She really must have been glad to see her!

"I can't believe you're really here!" Nancy exclaimed. "How did you manage to come on a Saturday afternoon?"

Mom sat on the couch beside Mary. "You know, our neighbors, the Goods, have a married son living just a few miles from here. They offered to bring us along in their van today as they came to visit their son and his family. Wasn't that nice of them? We can stay till tomorrow evening."

Nancy's eyes shone. This was too good to be true. "Are *Daed* (Dad) and the boys along, too?"

"Yes, Daed and Steven and Henry are, but not Joe and Omar. They stayed to do our chores, and anyhow, the van was full. The others are out in the barn with Jacob. We brought a picnic supper along, so there's nothing to prepare. We can sit and visit for awhile."

"How about *Maami* (Grandma)?" Nancy asked. "Is she hiding somewhere, too?"

"No, she's staying with Elam and Bertha," Mom replied, chuckling. "I knew it would make you sorry that she couldn't come, but she didn't feel up to it."

Mom got out the quilt patch she was appliqué-ing, and Mary worked on the afghan she had begun to crochet since her forced vacation. They believed in making use of every spare moment, so hands would never be idle when something useful could be done.

"You could take the little girls and go to gather the eggs," Mary suggested to Nancy. "I know you won't find many, but we want to be sure to have enough for our guests for breakfast tomorrow morning."

Nancy got the egg basket from the washhouse. "*Kummet, Meed* (come, girls)." She took Lydia by the hand.

"*Ich will geh Bieblin gucke* (I want to go see the chicks)," Lydia lisped.

"*Ya, Liebshdi* (yes, sweetheart)," Nancy crooned. It was so special seeing her little sisters again. "Tell me what all you've been doing," she said to Susie. "Did you help Mamm real well with the work?"

"Ya, I did." Susie was skipping along beside Nancy. "And Tabby has another nest of *Busslin* (kittens), and Omar got a new puppy!"

The barn door opened, and Nancy's brothers, Steven (fourteen) and Henry (ten), came out as the girls passed by on the way to the chicken house. Nancy felt so good to see them!

"How do you like it here?" Henry asked. "Does Jacob *retz* (tease) you a lot?"

"Ach, not much," Nancy told him. "I like to help him in the dairy barn. But they have a neighbor boy, Andrew Fisher, that likes to tease."

Nancy told them all about Andrew and Sally, the mystery supper, and the prank Andrew had played on her with the rubber snake.

"Humph!" Steven scoffed. "I'd fix him. I'd put a scorpion in his bed. It would serve him right to be stung."

But for some reason, Nancy did not like to hear Andrew being put down, so she changed the subject. "Let's go get the eggs," she told the little girls.

Steven and Henry strolled back into the barn. Dad and Jacob were looking at the horses and inspecting a quarter crack that King had in a hoof.

Henry looked around and suggested, "Let's see if we can chin ourselves on that pipe over there by the steer feed trough."

The boys raced over. Steven stood on the edge of the trough and swung himself up. His muscles bulged as his chin drew level with the bar. One, two, three.

Suddenly a small gold-colored object caught his eye, on the barn beam across from his eyes. He walked over on the trough edge, reached up, and took it down. "What's this?" he muttered. He opened his hand, and there in his palm lay the wristwatch with its gold band.

"*Guck mol do!* (look here once)," he exclaimed to Henry. "I found this on the barn beam."

"*Sunderbaar!* (strange)," Henry said excitedly. "That probably belonged to the people who lived here before Mary and Jacob took over."

"Hey, let's keep it," Steven murmured in a low voice. "I'm sure Mary and Jacob don't want it and didn't even know it was there." He slipped the watch into his pocket. "Now don't you go and tattle," he warned Henry.

"Ach, I'm not that *kindish* (childish)," Henry retorted. "*Ich loss die Katz net aus der Sack* (I won't let the cat out of the bag.)"

"Ya well, you'd better not!" Steven warned sternly.

Nancy and the little girls gathered the eggs and put them into the gas refrigerator. "Let's get our picnic ready now," Susie suggested eagerly. "Can we eat out by the creek?"

Mom laughed. "You now, too? I thought surely Nancy would be the one to suggest that."

"I don't believe I can walk that far," Mary said. "Why don't we just eat out in the yard?"

The girls ran out behind the house to find a good spot. "Here under the grape arbor, it's nice," Nancy planned. "We could carry the porch glider and the rockers back here."

The girls happily carried out the sandwiches, celery sticks, fruit, cookies, and half-moon pies. They arranged everything on the spread-out tablecloth. Mom brought the tureen of chicken corn soup she had reheated on the gas stove.

Dad, Jacob, and the boys were called from the barn, and they all seated themselves around the food.

This is too good to be true, Nancy thought joyously, *to have most of the family together again like this.*

They bowed their heads to ask the blessing, and peace and contentment filled her heart. Dad had smiled at her, tweaked her nose, and praised her for staying and helping Mary and Jacob. A few encouraging words like that always filled her with a desire to do better.

She, too, closed her eyes and whispered her thanks to *der Heiland* (the Savior) for the food, and for the blessing of having the family there.

Suddenly, there was an intruder in her peaceful thoughts. She remembered what she had done at the Baileys' house. Some of the happiness drained out of her. *Be sure your sin will find you out!* Did that apply to her, too, and not just to Aquila?

What would her parents think if they knew she had watched TV? What if they heard about the broken dish and the wristwatch she had hidden in the barn? They surely would not praise her then!

Nancy bowed her head in shame and in silent prayer asked for God's forgiveness. She resolved to confess to the Baileys about the dish and to give back the wristwatch. She would never even as much as glance at the Baileys' TV set again.

Then Nancy felt better. The blessing was over, and Mom began to pass out the food.

"Tomato sandwiches!" Nancy exclaimed. "I didn't know they were ripe yet."

"And homemade cup cheese," Susie piped up.

"Let's sing a song before we begin," Jacob suggested, and Nancy agreed. Now she felt like singing.

Jacob started the song, "*O Gott, mein Herr, wir danken dich, für alle gute Gaben* (O God, my Lord, we thank you for all good gifts)."

19

Morning Helpers

ON Sunday morning Nancy woke up wondering what it was that gave her the good, happy feeling in her heart. Then she saw Susie curled up in the bed beside her, and remembered.

She heard a banty rooster crowing outside, and a breeze flapped the blind at the window, revealing the sunrise in the east. Quickly she jumped out of bed. Today was church Sunday, and they had to hurry with the milking to make it to church on time. She quickly dressed, tiptoed past the sleeping Susie, and went downstairs.

Jacob sat on the couch putting on his shoes. "Well, well, you're up bright and early, without being called," he said in surprise. "I thought surely with

Steven and Henry here, you wouldn't need to help with the chores this morning."

"I want to anyway," Nancy assured him. "I like to work in the barn."

She skipped out the walk to the milk house. What a lovely morning it was! The cool breeze was so refreshing, and the sunrise was beautiful. There had been a rain shower during the night. Everything was washed clean and bright, and the birds sang joyously.

Nancy began to put together the milkers, and Jacob started the generator in the diesel shanty. A few minutes later, Dad and the boys came into the barn, too.

"I'll do this job for you, Nancy," Dad offered. "You have to do it all the rest of the time."

"Well, then I'll mix the milk replacer for the calves," Nancy replied.

She took the plastic buckets off the rack in the barn, filled them with the right amount of lukewarm water and scoops of milk replacer, and beat them with a wire whisk until all the lumps were dissolved.

Steven and Henry each grabbed two pails, and Nancy brought two more. They put them in the holders in front of the bawling, butting calves.

"They sure act hungry," Henry marveled. "As if they couldn't wait another minute to be fed."

They stood watching the eager calves gulping the milk replacer as fast as they could.

"Well, you know that if any of them wouldn't be hungry, they would surely be sick with the scours or something else just as bad," Steven pointed out.

"*Buwe* (boys)," Jacob called, "would you feed the horses for me so King will be finished feeding by the time we're ready to leave for church? We don't want to be late today."

The boys went to do his bidding. Nancy gathered the empty calf buckets and took them over to the sink tub to be washed. As she started rinsing the buckets, the milk house door opened, and Andrew came in.

He glanced into the dairy barn. "Your family is here for a visit, I see. Do you all have a way to go to church? I'm hitching old Barney to the two-seated carriage, and a few of you can go along if you want to. Dad and Mom and Sarah are going to church in the east district, so Sally and I will be the only ones in the carriage."

"The boys and I were planning to walk," Nancy replied. "Jacob's carriage will be full with Mamm and Daed and Mary and the little girls. But it's several miles to Sam's Sammie's Dave's place, where church services will be held today. I, for one, will sure be glad if I don't have to walk that far."

"All right. I'll drive over for you and your brothers," Andrew promised.

"Thank you," Nancy said warmly. "It was nice of you to offer to take us along."

Andrew returned her smile, went out the door, and kicked homeward on his scooter.

When the milking was finished, Nancy hurried with washing the milkers. Breakfast was probably being set out, and she wanted to make sure that she and the boys were ready when Andrew drove in, so he wouldn't have to wait.

The milk house door opened again, and Susie came in. "*Guten morgen* (good morning)," she greeted Nancy shyly. "Mamm said to tell you that breakfast is on, and that you can finish the milkers later."

"I'm all done now." Nancy dried her hands and took Susie's hand. "Let's go and eat."

Jacob and Dad and the boys were heading for the house, too.

Mmmm! Nancy wondered what smelled so good when she opened the kitchen door. Was it fresh brewed meadow tea and bacon and eggs?

Several boards had been put into the table to make it longer. A clean white tablecloth was spread over it, and it was set with Mary's pretty Sunday dishes with purple violets around the rim.

Dad seated himself at the head of the table, and Jacob handed him the family Bible. He began to read the Beatitudes.

Blessed are the poor in spirit,
  for theirs is the kingdom of heaven.
Blessed are they that mourn,
  for they shall be comforted.
Blessed are the meek,
  for they shall inherit the earth.
Blessed are they which do hunger and thirst
    after righteousness,
  for they shall be filled.
Blessed are the merciful,
  for they shall obtain mercy.

Blessed are the pure in heart,
for they shall see God.
Blessed are the peacemakers,
for they shall be called the children of God.

Nancy's soul felt bathed in peace and contentment as she listened to Dad's voice reading. *There's no place I'd rather be than with my family,* she thought. Although Joe and Omar were missing, she knew she would soon see them again. For now, this was enough.

"Let's bow our heads for prayer," Dad said.

During the silent prayer, Nancy listened to the ticking of the clock. She peeked at the food in front of her: a platter of steaming eggs and bacon, fried cornmeal mush, a bowl of hot cooked oatmeal, pitchers of creamy milk, and a cup of hot meadow tea at each plate. Guiltily Nancy squeezed her eyes shut.

"For health and strength and daily food, we praise thy name, O Lord," she whispered.

As soon as heads were raised again, Susie piped up, "I saw Nancy 'peepsing' (peeking) when she was supposed to have her eyes closed."

Nancy blushed a deep pink.

"How do you know?" Dad asked Susie. "You didn't see her beepsing, did you?"

"Yes, I did too," Susie retorted.

"You weren't beepsing yourself, were you?" he asked, pretending innocence.

The others began to laugh. "You just gave yourself away," Henry told her. "If you wouldn't have been peeking, you wouldn't have seen Nancy peek."

"*Yuscht glee bissel* (just a little bit)," Susie pouted.

"I think when Nancy goes home, I'll ask if I can have Susie," Mary said affectionately.

"*Mosch, Mosch, ich will Mosch!* (mush, I want mush)," Lydia was calling, banging her spoon on her plate.

Everything seems just like old times, Nancy thought. So dear and familiar!

Steven passed the platter of bacon and eggs to Henry, who took it with one hand.

"*Geb acht!* (take care). It's heavy," Dad warned.

But the platter had already tilted to the side, upsetting Henry's cup of tea.

"Ach my," Mom lamented. "On Mary's clean tablecloth, yet." She got up to find a rag for cleaning it up.

"I guess that means it will rain sometime today," Jacob teased.

"That's just an old saying," Steven countered. "It never holds up."

Suddenly Nancy realized how much she had missed the family's liveliness, the friendly bantering and laughter, the familiar chattering at the table. *Next I'll get a fresh dose of Heemweh when they leave,* she thought. *But I'll be brave and won't let anyone know it.*

20

An Unruly Horse

AFTER breakfast was over, Mom quickly washed the dishes. She had already combed Susie and made her bob and made Lydia's little hair bobbies (rolls) at the sides.

Nancy dried the dishes, put them away, and then slipped into the bathroom. After a quick scrubbing, she put on her Sunday dress and apron and began to do her hair. She had just learned to comb and put up her own hair this summer.

When she was finished, she looked at herself in the mirror as she put on her organdy *Kapp* (cap) and tied the strings. "I guess this will have to do," she murmured as she grabbed her bonnet.

Jacob and Dad were hitching King to the carriage. "I hope Andrew will be here for you soon," Mary remarked as she and Mom went out the door. "We don't want you to be late."

"I think he's coming in a few minutes," Nancy reassured her.

This was the first time Mary was going to church since her accident, so it was a special occasion. She could walk now, but still hobbled a bit.

Nancy stood at the window and watched as Mary headed for the carriage. *Mary looks plump,* she thought. *Maybe from sitting around so much, waiting for her leg to heal. Or is she going to have a baby?*

Mom, Mary, and the little girls climbed into the backseat. Then they raised the back of the front seat for Dad and Jacob.

King was prancing and dancing, as usual, eager to be off. With the rattle of wheels and flurry of flying gravel, they were off, heading out the lane.

Steven and Henry came into the house. "What's keeping that teaser friend of yours?" Steven wondered. "I hope he won't be late."

Nancy winced. She wished she had never said anything about Andrew being a teaser. "Why don't we walk over to Fishers and see what's keeping him," she suggested.

"Okay," Steven agreed. "Then he won't have to drive over for us."

At the end of Fishers' lane, they met an upset Andrew carrying the horse's bridle.

"Which way did that dumb *Esel* (mule) go?" he asked in exasperation. "Barney got away from me when I was trying to put on his bridle."

Sally came running around a corner of the barn, puffing and out of breath. "There he is!" she cried, pointing out across the field.

Sure enough, there was the runaway horse, calmly eating grass near the far fence, as if he hadn't a care in the world. The harness was on his back, but he apparently didn't want to be hitched up.

"*Ach du lieber!* (oh dear)," Andrew lamented. "We're in our Sunday clothes, and it just rained last night, so the field is muddy. How will we ever be able to chase Barney up here? And how can we make it to church on time?"

"I'll get you boys each a pair of *Schtiffel* (boots)," Sally offered. "Nancy and I will herd him toward the barn when he comes this way, and we'll have the barnyard gate open. We'll make it to church yet. Don't you worry!"

"Huh!" snorted Andrew. "*Du weescht net* (you don't know). I wonder if it's even worthwhile trying. He runs like a *Hasch* (deer). But, okay, let's go."

The three boys tramped down along the fencerow and tried to sneak past the horse to surround him.

Nancy and Sally watched from near the barn. "Terrible!" Sally exclaimed. "See how Barney has the *Bosheit* (mischief) in him! He's snorting and prancing wild-eyed even before they get close to him."

"There he goes!" Nancy yelled.

Old Barney lifted his tail high and took off at top speed.

"Stop him!" Andrew shouted.

Henry hollered and waved his arms but had to

jump aside at the last instant. Barney galloped free and upheaded off to the opposite side of the field.

"Ach my!" Sally lamented. "It's enough to make a person cry."

A minute later she cheered. "Hurrah! There goes Steven after him, and he's headed this way. If only he doesn't get a notion to turn around."

The girls watched breathlessly, hardly daring to hope. Barney had stopped now and was snorting and warily looking around.

"Let's stand back," Nancy suggested. "Maybe he'll decide to come this way then."

Sure enough, it worked.

"*Dapper!* (quick). Open the gate," she half whispered to Sally. "He's coming this way!"

Sally swung the gate open and stood back as Barney came thundering into the barnyard. "Three cheers!" she crowed as she closed the gate. "See, I was right! We'll still be in time for church."

Andrew, however, had other ideas when the boys came trudging in the lane. "I hate to be late for church," he complained. "Why don't we boys go for a swim instead?"

Sally's eyes flashed. "Andrew Fisher," she cried indignantly, stamping her foot, "you'll do no such thing! We aren't that late. You hitch up Barney this minute, and we'll all go to church at Sam's Sammie's Dave's place. Our families are expecting us there."

"Bossy sisters," Andrew muttered. "What would it matter to skip church just this once?" But he meekly led Barney to the carriage, and the boys hitched him up.

"Henry, you'll have to sit in the backseat with the girls," Steven ordered. "You're the youngest."

"I won't," Henry insisted stubbornly. "I'll sit on your lap in the front."

"Come, help me roll up the back curtain," Sally said to Nancy. "We'll need some fresh air, riding with three boys."

Nancy giggled.

"Okay, all aboard," Andrew called. "Let's go."

When they were at the end of the lane, Nancy cried out, "Please stop for a minute! I can hardly see because of the tree branches. But doesn't that look like a car in Jacob's driveway?"

All heads turned in that direction. "It sure is," Andrew agreed. "Want me to drive over and see who it is?"

"No, don't," Sally urged. "We're late so as it is, and we don't want to be later yet. It's probably just a tourist, wanting to ask directions. See, the man's back in the car now, and he's leaving. Go on!"

"Okay, whatever you say, boss," Andrew sassed. "Say, boys, you sure can be glad your sister isn't as bossy as mine is."

Nancy was only half listening. She twisted around to look over the back of the seat, trying to get a better view of the car. "It's blue, the same color blue as the Baileys' car," she observed. "But it wouldn't be them. They'd surely know better than to try to buy produce or butter on a Sunday."

Sally poked Nancy in the ribs. "Quit worrying about that car. We'd better keep an eye on the driver, or we'll end up in the *Graawe* (ditch). You're going too fast, Andrew. Slow down!" she called out.

"More bossing," Andrew muttered disgustedly. "No backseat driving allowed. Besides, I can't do much about it. Barney's worked up, and he would just like to run away again. I'm holding him back as hard as I can."

Barney picked up speed, and the carriage began to weave from side to side.

"Stop him!" Sally yelled.

Nancy was too frightened to move or speak. The carriage went around a bend in the road on two wheels. Even Andrew was scared now.

"*Helfet, Buwe!* (help, boys)," he cried. "Pull on the lines with me!"

Steven grabbed hold of the lines in front of Andrew's hands, and together they soon had the horse under control again.

"Now if Sally doesn't yell too much, we should be able to keep Barney on the road." Andrew tried to shift the blame and gave his sister a dark look. "But at least we'll get there faster this way."

To Nancy, it seemed only a few minutes later that they were pulling into the lane at Dave's, where church services were being held. As soon as the carriage stopped, Nancy jumped out. She suddenly realized that her knees were weak and trembling.

"I think maybe I'll walk home after church," she whispered to Sally. "I didn't know Barney was such a handful."

"It's just because he was stirred up from running away this morning," Sally replied. "Maybe by this afternoon he'll have forgotten it. He's usually okay."

21

The Watchdog

AFTER church services were over, Sally, Barbie, and Nancy went outside for a breath of fresh air. The men were setting up tables and benches in the kitchen and *Sitzschtupp* (sitting room). The women were busy getting the food ready for the table.

"How did it seem to have your parents and brothers and sisters here?" Barbie asked Nancy. "Maybe almost like church services at home?"

"*Wunderbaar shee* (wonderfully nice)," Nancy replied. "But Mom was going to let little Lydia sit with me, and I was disappointed that she couldn't because we were late."

"Well, let's go and find *Buppelin* (babies) to hold," Sally said. The girls went back into the house.

In the kitchen, the women were setting the tables already. They put on plates of homemade bread and rolls, red beets, pickles, cup cheese, dishes of church spread (a mixture of peanut butter and molasses), *Schnitzboi* (dried-apple pie), and cups of steaming hot coffee and tea.

"Let's wait until we've eaten dinner," Nancy suggested. "The *Memm* (moms) want to feed their babies first, too, before they hand them to us girls."

After dinner the girls each chose a *Buppeli* and its *Kaerwli* (diaper basket) and went out to sit on the porch swing. But it was already crowded.

"Of course, it's full of little girls," Barbie griped. "Let's go down to the creek and sit on its bank."

"Are you sure there's no bull in the meadow?" Nancy asked. She said *bull*, but actually she was thinking more about snakes.

"Ach no. Dave's don't have a bull," Sally told her. "And the cows are way back in the other end of the meadow. Let's go."

The baby that Nancy was carrying was a *schnuck* (cute) little girl about ten months old, with two little bobbies on either side of her head above her face. The girls walked past a boy of *rumschpringing* age who was hitching his horse to his buggy to go home. "*Gauli, Gauli* (horsie)," cried the baby, jumping up and down in Nancy's arms.

The boy looked at them and smiled. He reached over and patted the baby on the head.

"That's my *gleene Schweschder* (little sister)," he said. "Be sure you don't drop her."

The girls giggled and walked on. Barbie opened

the meadow gate with one arm, carrying her baby on her hip.

"Oh no!" Sally groaned. "There's Andrew and his gang down by the creek. Let's not sit close to them."

"Here's a nice spot under this big *Schaddebaam* (shade tree)," Barbie proposed. "There are a few big rocks to sit on, too. It's plenty close enough to the boys, but we'll turn our backs to them."

The boys were talking loudly, and the girls could hear every word they were saying. Nancy noticed that Steven and Henry were with the bigger boys but not the center of attention like Andrew was.

"Your dog isn't worth anything," he was saying loudly to Dave's Sammie. "*Nixwaert! Nixwaert!* (worthless)," he began to chant. "Why, he'd even be afraid of his own shadow. Even a flying insect could chase him."

"That's what you think!" Sammie retorted angrily. "I have Buster tied up, but if I'd let him loose and sic him on you, you'd soon be minus a leg!"

"Humph!" Andrew scoffed. "All I'd have to do would be to snap my fingers, and he'd turn and head for the barn as fast as he could, with his tail between his legs!"

"Ach, that terrible Andrew," Sally moaned in disgust. "I wish those boys would go somewhere else."

Sammie whispered something to his younger brother, Abie, who got up and headed for the barn. Andrew, sitting with his back against a rock and throwing stones into the creek, didn't see Abie leave.

"Buster is one of the best watchdogs we ever

had," Sammie went on, trying to bait Andrew some more.

"*Nixwaert! Nixwaert!*" Andrew chanted again. "Buster's bark doesn't mean a thing. If even a butterfly would land on his head, he'd go and hide under the porch.

"No, even just a louse would do it," Andrew mocked. "A louse on the end of his tail would send him off yelping."

The other boys roared with laughter.

"Andrew!" Sally could be quiet no longer. "I'm going to tell Dad on you!"

"Tattletale, tattletale, hanging on a bull's tail," Andrew chanted.

Nancy looked back and saw that Abie was coming with Buster on a chain.

Sammie grabbed the chain and cried, "Step back, boys. We're going to make Andrew eat his words.

"*Hiss! Hetz ihn!* (sic him), Buster," he commanded, setting the dog on Andrew.

Andrew jumped up, yelling, and began to swing his fists menacingly at the dog. That angered Buster even more.

"*Hiss! Hetz ihn! Hiss! Hetz ihn!*" Sammie urged again.

Buster growled deeply and began to advance on Andrew with his teeth bared.

Slowly Andrew backed away until he was under a big willow tree partly overhanging the creek. Quick as a flash he swung himself up onto a branch, just as the dog sprang at him.

Sammie circled the dog's chain around the tree trunk and snapped it fast. "Ho ho ho!" he cheered. "Now we'll let you think over what all you said. C'mon, boys, let's go up to the barn and let Andrew chew his cud for awhile."

"Steven, Henry!" Andrew called. "If you boys want to go home with me, you'd better get that dog and lead him to the barn."

Steven and Henry stopped and turned back. They didn't know any of these boys very well yet. But the brothers decided that since they wanted to go home with Andrew, they might as well side with him.

"Here, Buster," Steven invited, holding out his hand and trying to befriend the dog.

But Buster was thoroughly *hetzed* up by now, and he sprang at Steven with a growl and bared teeth.

"C'mon, boys," Sammie gloated. "Let him think over things for awhile. Maybe after this he'll use his head before he flaps his tongue."

"It serves you right, Andrew," Sally called to him. "There's no better way to teach you a lesson."

Nancy felt a stab of sympathy for Andrew, but she knew that Sally was right. Andrew would be a fine boy if he could overcome some of his *grosshunsich* (smart-alecky) ways. Maybe this would take some of it out of him.

The girls went on playing with their little "dolls" and ignored Andrew. He knew it was useless to ask the girls to remove the dog, so he just sat there with bowed head.

After awhile the boys came back. "Are you ready to come down?" Sammie called. "If you say Buster is the finest watchdog you know, I'll let you down."

But Andrew wasn't broken yet. "Who says I want to come down?" he asked tartly. "I like it up here. It's nice and cool. The only thing that isn't so nice is being so near such a worthless cur." He stretched out on a large branch and pretended to be napping.

Without a word, Sammie turned on his heel, and the boys followed him back to the barn.

Sally nearly had a fit. "Ei yi yi!" she gasped in amazement. "The longer he waits to back down, the harder it'll be for him to swallow his pride. He hasn't learned his lesson yet. I sure hope he gives himself up before it's time to go home."

One by one the babies dropped off to sleep. "My arms are getting tired," complained Barbie after awhile. "I'm ready to go back to the house."

"Mine are too," Sally agreed. "But I'd sure like to be here to see Andrew give in and swallow his pride. It would be the best thing I ever heard. It would be worth waiting here all afternoon to hear it."

"Maybe he fell asleep," Nancy suggested. But then she saw the boys coming back.

"The people are leaving," Sammie told Andrew. "How soon are you ready to come down? All you have to do is say that Buster is the best watchdog you ever saw. Then I'll take him back to the barn."

"All right, I'll say it," Andrew agreed.

"Okay, but you'll have to say it in exactly the same words," Sammie instructed. "Say it loud and clear."

Andrew got a mischievous look on his face. "Buster is the best watchdog *you* ever saw," he said, grinning.

In exasperation Sammie stamped his foot. "All right, c'mon, boys. He's not ready yet."

"What's going on here?" a deep voice behind them demanded. It was Dave, the dad of Sammie and Abie. "Sammie, you take the dog up to the barn this minute."

Sammie knew that it was useless to argue. Meekly and with great disappointment on his face, he unsnapped Buster's chain from the tree and led him back to the barn.

Andrew laughed triumphantly, "*Da wer es letscht lacht, lacht bescht* (whoever laughs last, laughs best)," he crowed. But he knew it was high time to clear out.

"I'm hitching up right now," he told Steven, Henry, and the girls. "Get ready to leave."

"It's too bad Dave showed up when he did," Sally groused as the girls walked to the house with their sleeping *Buppelin*. "I sure would've enjoyed hearing Andrew swallow his pride and eat his words."

"He'll learn his lesson sometime," Barbie predicted. "He can't always come out on top."

None of the girls realized how soon Andrew would come out on the bottom, and they with him.

22

Race for Home

As they climbed into the carriage to leave, Barney was just like he had been in the morning, restless, eager, and rarin' to be off.

"Hold onto your bonnets, girls," Andrew said to Nancy and Sally on the backseat. "We're really going to fly. Old Barney got a taste of what it's like to run off this morning, and he's going to try it again."

"Ach, Andrew, I wouldn't be surprised if you'd do it on purpose," Sally scolded. "Now act decent once, and drive like you should."

"What do you mean?" Andrew pretended to be hurt. "I can't help it if Barney holds hard and tries to run away. He wants to get home and have some oats. Steven will just have to help hold him back again if he gets out of hand."

The first mile and a half was covered in record time, with Barney traveling fast, but not too fast. Then Andrew spied Deacon Miller up ahead. He was still smarting a bit from the rebuke the deacon had given him when he had played a prank in church.

"There goes old Deacon Miller," he told the others. "I'd know his horse anywhere. I'll show him a thing or two."

"Don't you dare, Andrew!" Sally warned him. "You'll *mache Dummheit* (reach stupidity) yet."

"What do you mean?" Andrew retorted. "I can't help it that Barney goes faster than the deacon's pokey old horse. I'm not making him go faster."

"But you're slackening your hold on the reins, and you know it!" Sally accused him hotly. "What if you can't control Barney when you're trying to pass? We could end up in the ditch! Deacon Miller's horse is going real fast, too, if I know anything."

"Stop yelling, sis. You're getting Barney all excited."

Barney was picking up speed, and the distance between the two carriages was closing. Their carriage began to sway ever so slightly.

"Help him hold back, Steven," Nancy urged her brother.

"Now wait a minute," Andrew protested. "After we've passed him, you can help pull on the reins. But not now. I'm going to pass. You can count on that."

Soon the two carriages were side by side, and the horses were stirring each other up and competing.

"Their horse is galloping, and it looks like they can't control him," Sally moaned as she looked out the little side window. "Andrew, you'll *mache Dummheit* yet for sure, racing with the deacon like this!"

Doesn't Andrew remember what happened when he passed us and the spring wagon seat flipped over backward? Nancy thought in dismay.

Barney was pulling ahead now, and Andrew crowed, "We won! We won! We did it! Okay, Steven, pull on the reins now, and help me to slow Barney down."

Suddenly they hit a bump in the road. There was a sharp crack and a thud. The reins were jerked out of Andrew's hands. The front end of the carriage bumped to the ground, then the whole thing rolled over on its side and landed on its top.

Nancy was thrown against Sally and flipped upside down.

Then all was still.

"*Ach du leiber!* (oh dear)," Anna Miller cried, close to tears.

Her husband quickly slowed his horse to a stop and tied him to the fence.

Old Barney was running away down the road at top speed, his harness tugging the shafts still attached to the two front carriage wheels.

"*Ach, mei Zeit!* (oh, how awful)," Anna Miller moaned again. "What if they are hurt or killed!"

The dust was settling around the overturned carriage, and everything remained quiet for a few moments. Then one carriage door was pushed open, and Andrew poked his head out. He crawled out, apparently unhurt. One by one, the others all climbed out, bewildered and shaken.

Deacon Miller sadly shook his head. "Andrew, I'm sorry you had a wreck and that you *Buwe un Meed* were jolted around so badly.

"But, well, it seems to me, *sell . . . sell . . . sell is was du griegst* (that's what you get) for driving so fast and recklessly. You were asking for *Druwwel* (trouble), in my opinion."

Andrew hung his head in dismay. With a sinking heart, he watched Barney and the two front wheels disappear around a bend in the road. "I—I can't understand what happened," he muttered.

Deacon Miller walked over to the front of the carriage. "See here," he pointed out. "It looks like the kingpin jolted out of the fifth wheel on the front axle. That's how you lost your two front wheels. If you walk back the road a piece, you might find the pin.

"It will seem like a miracle if your horse runs home the rest of the way without being hit by a car. Well, let's pull your wreck off the road, and then we'll take you home."

"The girls can go with you, but the boys and I will walk."

Several of them grabbed the smashed carriage and dragged it partly into the ditch so it wouldn't block the road. Henry ran back to the bump and found the kingpin at the side of the road.

It was a sober and subdued Andrew who walked homeward, with plenty of time to think things over.

Sally and Nancy climbed into the backseat of the Miller carriage. Nancy's knees were still shaking, and she felt weak all over.

"Nancy!" Sally cried in alarm. "Your mouth is bleeding! You must have cut your lips."

Nancy got her handkerchief and dabbed at her lips. She had felt no pain until now. Then she looked at Sally and reported what she saw. "There's a scratch on your arm and a rip in your apron."

"Tsk tsk," Deacon Miller responded. "Haste makes waste. It doesn't pay to be *schusslich* (in a careless hurry)."

"I hope Andrew learned his lesson," Sally declared. "We told him not to try to pass you."

"So often it's that way," Deacon Miller stated. "The innocent suffer with the guilty. Tsk tsk."

While the boys were walking homeward, Henry discovered that his nose was bleeding. Andrew felt his left arm paining him severely. Steven had a scratch on his face and a bump on his head.

They were close to home when Jacob caught up to them with his carriage load.

"Whoa," Jacob ordered King. "*Was in die welt* (what in the world) happened to you?" he asked in amazement.

"What a pitiful sight!" Mary cried. "Look at Andrew's arm!"

"Yes, it's swollen," observed Dad. "I wonder if it's broken."

In the shock of the accident, no one had noticed how bad the arm was.

"Pile in, all of you," Jacob directed. He pulled the

little bench out from under the seat for Andrew to sit on, and Henry sat on Dad's lap. Steven sat on the floor with his feet on the carriage step.

"We'll stop to see if Mrs. Davis can take Andrew to the doctor," Jacob decided.

Dad agreed. "This arm sure needs attention right away. Now, boys, out with it once. What happened?"

"Didn't you see the upside-down carriage back there?" Steven asked, motioning in the direction of where the accident happened.

"Why no. We took the long way around, past the stone quarry," Jacob explained. "Was it wrecked?"

"I'll let Andrew tell you," Steven said.

Andrew hung his head. "My arm hurts too much to talk. Sally and Nancy can tell you when we get home. It was my fault, though," he admitted meekly. "I'm sorry. I'll try to do better."

It was too bad that Sally wasn't along to hear his sincere confession.

23

Stolen Bible

IT was after supper and the chores were all finished. On the front porch, Dad and Jacob were visiting. Steven and Henry were playing a game of checkers at the porch steps.

In the yard, Susie and Lydia were playing with Mary's *Lumbebopp* (rag doll). Mom, Mary, and Nancy were talking as they straightened up the kitchen.

The door opened and Sally came in. "Andrew's home," she announced, out of breath from running. "He has his arm bandaged. They x-rayed it and said it was badly sprained but not broken.

"He has to have it in a sling for a few days. The pain is *wunderbaar*. As soon as he got home, he took pain pills and went right to bed."

"Well, I guess we can be *dankbaar* (thankful) that it wasn't worse," Mom commented. "It's nothing that can't be fixed."

"How's Barney?" Nancy wondered. "Did he hurt himself any?"

"Not a *Gratz* (scratch)," Sally replied. "He ran right up to the barn door and stood there until Dad unhitched him and put him in the barn. I guess he knew that he had raised enough *Bosheit* (mischief) for one day."

"All's well that ends well," Mary commented practically. "What did your dad say when he heard the story, how it happened, and all?"

"Well, he was sorry that Andrew got hurt. But he said it was high time that Andrew was taken down a peg or two.

"I guess it could have happened anytime to anybody, but I think Andrew learned a lot because it happened just then," Sally added with a twinkle in her eyes.

Dad and Jacob came into the kitchen. "What time did you say the Goods are stopping in for us tonight?" he asked Mom.

"Around eight o'clock," she replied. "They should be here soon."

Mary struggled to her feet. "Ach ya, before you go, I want to show you the new secretary desk Jacob bought for me." She led the way, limping into the *Sitzschtupp* (sitting room).

Mom and Dad admired the beautiful old piece of cherry furniture.

"You couldn't guess what we found in a drawer

of the desk," Jacob told them, smiling. "A valuable old Froschauer Bible. Here, I'll show it to you."

He opened the slanted desk front and pulled out the secret drawer. "Where did you put that Bible, Mary?" he asked in a puzzled voice. "It's not in here."

"I didn't move it," Mary answered. "Nancy, did you put it somewhere?"

"*Nee, ich hab net* (no, I didn't)," Nancy said emphatically. "I don't think I touched it since the day we got it."

"Well, that's strange," Jacob muttered. He began to pull open drawer after drawer, searching for the missing Bible. "Where could it be?" he asked, scratching his head. "Maybe I just mislaid it."

He went on to tell Mom and Dad Petersheim how they had found the Bible in the desk, Mr. Bailey had offered $400.00 for it, and he had declined the offer.

"Are you sure it's not *gschtohle* (stolen) then," Dad asked, "if it's so valuable?"

"I sure hope not!" Jacob exclaimed. "I was looking through it yesterday before you came. Maybe in my hurry to go out and meet you, I just mislaid it somewhere. It spites me that I can't show it to you."

"Ya well," Dad soothed Jacob and Mary, "no matter how valuable any special edition, it is the words of the Bible that are priceless and worth more than any amount of money.

"We're thankful that we have religious freedom and are allowed to have God's Word in our homes. We want to be sure that we store it in our hearts and not just on the shelf."

"That's true, for sure," Jacob agreed. "It would be a pity if we would just have the Bible as a heirloom and did not heed the message inside."

"Well, the Goods just drove in now," Mom informed them. "We don't want to make them wait. Maybe we can see the Bible the next time we come."

"Say, Mary, you're not letting Nancy go along home are you?" Jacob asked his wife. "We sure need her in the dairy barn yet."

"No. She's staying until September first." Mary smiled at Nancy. "I need her, too, to run errands. I hope she doesn't get *Heemweh* when the others leave."

Nancy assured them she would not. But when the family began to walk out the door, she discovered a lump in her throat that she couldn't swallow, and tears pushed at her eyelids. *It's just until they're gone, and then I'll get over it,* she told herself.

"Bye, Nancy, bye-bye," Susie and Lydia were calling and waving.

"Good-bye, girls," Nancy called back, forcing a smile. "Be good girls, and wash the dishes for Mom."

Mom clasped Nancy's hand and smiled. She was glad to see that Nancy was taking the parting so well. Mom knew her strong feelings for home. She remembered how Nancy had pined away when she was afraid that Dad would sell their dear Whispering Brook Farm, as Nancy named it.

Maybe Nancy's growing up, Mom thought fondly. *She's learning to stand on her own two feet.*

"Say hi to Maami for me," Nancy said. "I wish she could've come along, too."

"We will," Mom promised. "We'll tell her you sent a greeting along for her."

Nancy watched as the van full of family headed out the lane. She waved until they were out of sight. Then she swallowed hard and wiped away a few tears.

"Let's walk out to the bridge" came from a voice at her elbow.

Nancy jumped. "Oh, Sally, I forgot you were here." She laughed shakily. "Yes, let's do that." Together they strolled down the road.

"Do you still want me to go with you to your cleaning job on Wednesday?" Sally wondered.

"Yes, please do!" Nancy begged. "I won't go if you don't come along."

"All right, I will. But why don't you want to go alone?"

"I just don't want to," Nancy hedged. "I'll feel better if you're along."

She was silent for a bit and then decided to trust Sally with her secret. "They had their TV on when I was there, and I happened to drop and break a *Schissel* (dish) I was dusting. I thought I'd give them one of Mary's dishes that looks like the one I broke, so I quickly took the broken pieces outside and buried them. Now I think I should tell them what happened."

Sally began to laugh. "Ach, Nancy, you're more daring than I thought you'd be."

"I'm not daring," Nancy protested. "I think I'm a

coward. Why was I so *dumm* (dumb)?"

"Well, I think you should let it go now," Sally advised. "The Baileys are rich, and they have lots of dishes. Just forget about it. They probably never noticed that it was missing."

"Well, all right," Nancy agreed reluctantly. "But I do want to replace the dish. Let's go ask Mary right now about her *Schissel* that matches. It's in the kitchen hutch."

The girls ran back to the house. Mary and Jacob were sitting on the porch glider. Nancy got the dish and showed it to Mary.

"Where did you get this dish?" she asked. "You wouldn't want to part with it, would you?"

"Oh that!" Mary chuckled. "I got that at a yard sale for a dollar or two. If you want it, you can have it. Is it for your hope chest?"

"Just for nice," Nancy replied lamely. "*Danki* (thank you) for it."

"*Gern gschehne* (you're welcome)."

The girls ran upstairs to Nancy's room. "Maybe on Wednesday we can hide it under my apron when we get to the Baileys," Nancy suggested. "If I put it in a bag, Mrs. Bailey will ask me what I have."

"If you hide it under your apron, Mrs. Bailey will wonder how you got so fat." Sally giggled.

Suddenly Nancy stopped in her tracks. "Sally," she cried, "remember the car we saw in Jacob's lane this morning when we started out from your place? I'm pretty sure that was the Baileys' car. Do you think that's why the old Bible is missing? Mr. Bailey was so determined to buy it from Jacob. He said if

Jacob didn't sell it to him, he would wish he had."

"Whew!" Sally whistled. "That sure makes him look suspicious."

"Let's go hunt for the Bible again," Nancy suggested eagerly. "We don't need to tell Mary and Jacob that we saw that car. We'll do some detective work of our own.

"If the Bible really is stolen, maybe when we go to clean for the Baileys, we can hunt for it there when they go out to buy lunch. I know where they keep their valuable books."

"Say, that's a good idea!" Sally was enthusiastic. "Let's go!"

They went downstairs and hunted for a full half hour for the old Bible, in the parlor, in the sitting room, and in the kitchen—everywhere they could imagine that a Bible could possibly be.

"Ya well, I'm sure it's not in this house!" Nancy finally declared. "We've looked everywhere."

"I agree. If I'd be allowed to bet, I'd bet my bottom dollar that Mr. Bailey stole the Bible."

Nancy was shocked. "Don't even talk like that, Sally," she scolded. "Betting is wrong."

Sally shrugged. "Oh, I don't bet. I just learned that expression from Andrew. But you know, even though we're sure that Mr. Bailey stole the Bible, there's not a thing we can do unless we have proof. I sure will help you try to prove it.

"I've got to go now, but I'll see you on Wednesday, and if possible, we'll get that Bible back. It's a mighty slim chance, but we'll do our best."

"We sure will," Nancy agreed. "Jacob didn't sell

the Bible after I said antiques get more valuable over time. So I feel responsible. Let's try to get it back."

"We just might be able to do that," Sally responded hopefully. "I'll see you on Wednesday, then."

Nancy watched as Sally skipped homeward. *I forgot all about being Heemweh,* she thought. *Planning to be a detective is lots of fun. I sure hope we'll be able to accomplish something.*

24

Amish Thieves

ON Monday morning after breakfast, Mary and Jacob hunted for the old German Bible again, without success. Finally they gave it up.

"There's no doubt in my mind who took it," Jacob mused. "But since I have no proof, I can't do anything about it. I've known Mr. Bailey for awhile now, and I never would have taken him for a *Dieb* (thief)."

"Are you going to report it to the police?" Nancy asked.

"Well, *ich denk net* (I guess not)," Jacob decided. "I don't think there's anything the police could do to get it back for us. Besides, maybe the old Bible never really belonged to us anyway."

Secretly, Nancy was glad. She and Sally were planning to be detectives and solve this mystery themselves! Instead of dreading her Wednesday cleaning job, she was feeling excited about it.

She had her candy dish ready, and Sally would be with her. That would make a big difference. Already she had forgotten her resolution to return the wristwatch and to confess about the broken dish.

On Wednesday morning Sally came over to Jacob and Mary's house to wait until Mrs. Bailey came for them.

"Where did you hide the dish?" she whispered to Nancy, so Mary wouldn't hear.

"In my slip," Nancy whispered back, giggling. "I looped up the bottom of it in the front to make a pocket and put safety pins all around. Now I'll have to be careful I don't bump it against anything when I walk, or it'll break."

Sally began to giggle helplessly. "You'll have to walk like an old *Maami* (grandma)," she squealed.

"Shhh!" Nancy scolded. "Next Mary will hear you and wonder what we're up to."

"There comes Mrs. Bailey now." Sally jumped up. "Now be careful when you climb in the car. I'll open the door for you."

Nancy gingerly slipped into the back seat of the car, clutching at her clothes so the dish wouldn't bang against the door frame. Sally got in on the other side.

"Well, well, two of you today!" Mrs. Bailey exclaimed. "That means we'll really get a lot of cleaning done. Mr. Bailey went to an auction today, so we'll have the house to ourselves. What's your friend's name, Nancy?"

Nancy introduced Sally, then settled back into the soft, plush seat with a sigh of relief. She was glad that Mr. Bailey wasn't home. It would be easier to put the dish into place and to hunt for the Bible.

In a few minutes they pulled into the Baileys' garage, with its automatic door opener. *Englischers have it so nice,* Nancy mused. *They have everything air-conditioned, even their cars. They never get cranky from the heat.*

They don't have to work as hard either. Not much kitchen cleanup since they just put things in the dishwasher. Pampers for babies, so no dirty diapers to clean. Food from supermarkets or in restaurants, so no hot canning in the summer. They don't have to do anything they dread!

Nancy's reverie was cut short by Sally whispering in her ear, "Be careful when you get out of the car."

Nancy nodded. She surely didn't want to break her dish.

"I'm really glad that there are two of you today," Mrs. Bailey said. "I have an appointment at the hairdresser. Then I want to do a bit of shopping. Mr. Bailey won't get back from the auction before late afternoon.

"I'll just show you what I want done. Nancy, you know how to go ahead with the work, don't you?"

"Oh yes," Nancy replied.

This was too good to be true! Having the house to themselves was just what they wanted.

Mrs. Bailey started the girls at cleaning the balcony room, then settled down in the family room to watch television until it was time to leave. Nancy and Sally whispered together excitedly as they dusted the trophies and books on the shelves. It was so much more fun cleaning with a friend than alone.

After awhile, Nancy checked to make sure that Mrs. Bailey wasn't watching. She walked over to Mr. Bailey's bookcase storing the valuable volumes, knelt, and cupped both hands against the glass front to cut the reflections while she peered inside. To her dismay, all she could see was a blur of rows and rows of books.

"Ach," she whispered to Sally, "the glass has been frosted! I can't see much at all. It wasn't that way last week!"

"That proves it!" Sally declared.

All of a sudden, Nancy remembered the key she had seen in the ceramic turtle. She cast a nervous glance down into the family room, where Mrs. Bailey, with her back to them, was watching television. Then she motioned to Sally to come and see. Without making a noise, Nancy lifted the turtle's lid.

"It's gone!" she whispered in dismay. "Last week there was a key inside, but now it's empty. I'm sure that was the key to the bookcase."

She carefully put the lid back on and began vigorously to dust the top of the desk.

"*Sell veist, das die Biewel drin is!* (that shows that the Bible is in there)," Sally declared emphatically.

Nancy nodded. What a disappointment! She swung around to dust a high shelf and heard a telltale thud.

"*Ach mei, mei Schissel!* (oh my, my dish)," she gasped, her eyes wide. "I forgot all about it, and it bumped against that stand. It's probably broken in half!"

"*Du dumm Ding!* (you dumb thing)," Sally scolded.

"What are you girls whispering about?" The voice was at Sally's elbow.

Both girls jumped.

"Ach, Mrs. Bailey, you scared me so!" Sally gasped. She laughed at the German word she had used by mistake. "I didn't hear you coming."

"Well, you don't need to whisper," Mrs. Bailey said. "You can talk out loud. I'm ready to leave now, and I'll be back in time to bring you some lunch. I'll see you in a few hours."

The girls worked in silence until they heard the outside door closing.

"How did she come up here so fast without us hearing her?" Nancy wondered. "I'm sure glad we weren't peeking into the bookcase or the turtle just then."

"On this carpet, people can sure sneak around," Sally replied. "But what about your dish? Is it broken?"

"I'll find out in a minute." Nancy bent over and lifted her dress. One by one she took the safety pins out of her petticoat. "Here it is, safe and sound," she cried triumphantly.

Sally reached for the dish and examined it closely. "Not even a nick or a crack," she observed.

Nancy took the dish down to the family room

and put it on the table where the dish she had broken had been. "There! Now that's safely done. But Sally, do you think it's right? Shouldn't I tell Mrs. Bailey that I broke her dish?"

"*Nee!*" Sally responded casually. "You've replaced it, so you're even. And if Mr. Bailey stole your Bible, you sure needn't worry about that little dish. Do you think it's worth our time to hunt for the Bible now that she's gone?"

"No, I don't think so," Nancy replied. "I'd be willing to bet—oops, Sally, now look what I learned from you!"

Sally giggled.

Nancy went on, "I mean, I'm really sure that the Bible is locked inside Mr. Bailey's bookcase, and there's no way we can get it out."

"Not unless we break the glass," Sally said matter-of-factly.

But the girls both knew they wouldn't dare to do that. They went up to the balcony room and tried the door to the bookcase again. It was certainly locked.

"That makes me mad," Sally sighed. "So near to it and yet so far. But let's work fast and get the cleaning done in a hurry anyway."

Nancy was standing on a chair dusting a chandelier when she spied a shiny object in the large hanging-basket planter a few feet away from her. It was barely visible among the green vines, but Nancy knew right away it was the key to the bookcase.

"*Der Schlissel!* (the key)," she cried. "Sally, *mach schnell, kumm, ich hab der Schlissel gfunne!* (come quickly, I've found the key)."

Quickly she brushed the dirt off the key and inserted it into the lock. Sally was at her elbow, eagerly waiting to see what was inside.

The door swung open. "There's the Froschauer Bible!" Sally murmured in an awed voice. She took the Bible down and opened it. "Isn't that the same writing there in the front that was in your Bible?"

"It sure looks the same to me," Nancy replied. "But I really didn't pay much attention to that part."

"Well, I'd be willing to bet . . . er, I mean I'm 99 percent sure it's your Bible. Let's take it."

"I—I don't know," Nancy said weakly. "What if it isn't the same one? We'd get ourselves into an awful lot of trouble."

"Of course it's the same one," Sally insisted. "We saw Mr. Bailey in Jacob's lane, didn't we? And Jacob's Bible is missing."

Suddenly the girls froze. Someone was coming! The doorbell was ringing!

Quick as a flash, Sally hid the Bible under the cushions on the davenport. Nancy locked the bookcase door and put the key back into the planter. Her hands were trembling badly.

25

Wanted!

IT was only the milkman, but it left the girls badly frightened. After he dropped off the ordered milk and cheese, Nancy said in a worried voice, "Sally, *wie in de Welt* (how in the world) are we going to get this Bible home? There's no way we can take it without Mrs. Bailey seeing it and asking what we have."

"I have it all figured out." Sally gloated. "I'll put the Bible in a plastic bag, run out the road a piece with it, and hide it under the honeysuckle vines. Then this afternoon I'll come by with the pony and wagon, wrap it in a blanket, and take it home."

"I don't know. What if someone would see you?"

"Ach, just quit worrying once, Nancy," Sally

scolded. "This is a quiet road. Here, I found a plastic bag in the trash can, and I'm ready to wrap the Bible."

"Well, hurry then," Nancy urged. "It would be too bad if Mrs. Bailey came back just when you're going out the door with it."

Nancy was jittery until Sally came running back.

"I found the perfect hiding place," she cried, laughing and breathless. "It's covered with vines and dead leaves. But I stuck a small branch upright there so I can easily find it again."

Nancy heaved a sigh of relief. But she still had a

guilty feeling inside. Somehow, it didn't seem to be right. But Sally was so sure.

"How did you find the key?" Sally wondered.

When Nancy explained, Sally began to laugh. "Did you really stand on one of those valuable antique chairs? Mrs. Bailey would've had a fit if she'd seen you! How did you clean the chandelier last week?"

"I didn't," Nancy admitted. "Mrs. Bailey had me dusting other things. But today I noticed that it didn't shine right."

"Well, it's lucky you cleaned it. There's no other way we'd have found the key."

When Mrs. Bailey returned with hamburgers and french fries for lunch, the girls were nearly done with the cleaning, even the windows.

"You girls are fantastic!" she gushed. "I think I'll get you to scrub the kitchen floor yet after lunch. Then we'll be finished for the day. I'll have your lunch ready in a jiffy."

Those hamburgers, fries, and milkshakes didn't taste very good to Nancy. They seemed like sawdust and stuck in her throat. She wondered if Sally felt as guilty and uneasy about taking the Bible.

She couldn't face Mrs. Bailey and avoided direct eye contact with her. It was a great relief to her when Mrs. Bailey finally said they were finished and that she was ready to take them home.

All kinds of thoughts were tumbling over each other in Nancy's mind. What if some field mice or moles chewed on the Bible's pages? What if a passing bicyclist found it and took it away?

When Mrs. Bailey dropped the girls off at the end of Jacob's lane, Sally quickly ran home and hitched Maggie to the spring wagon. In a short time she was back, whistling for Nancy to go along.

"I'm sorry, but I can't go," Nancy apologized. "Mary asked me to weed the garden this afternoon. Do you think you can manage alone?"

"Sure I can. I've got the carriage blanket here. I'll take the Bible along to my home and bring it over here right after dark tonight so no one will see it. Meet me at the end of the lane then."

Nancy's thoughts were troubled as she went back to her weeding. She wished with all her heart that she had never found that key.

The sun's rays beat mercilessly on her back, and she wanted to go and lie down in the shade. After awhile, she got herself a drink of cool water at the pump and poured some over her dusty bare feet to cool them.

Then she found the hoe in the washhouse and chopped weeds out of the corn rows until her arms and back ached. *Surely it must be about supper time,* she thought wistfully, pushing back her *struwwels* (loose strands of hair).

Suddenly Nancy opened her eyes wide, then blinked in surprise. Was she dreaming, or was that a police car coming in Jacob's lane?

With a dry sob, she threw down her hoe, wondering wildly which way she could run. Just below the garden was the springhouse, where Mary kept cream to make butter. A spring flowed through it, and years ago before there were refrigerators, it had kept all the perishable foodstuffs cool.

As soon as the police car disappeared between house and barn, Nancy made a dash for it, dived in the springhouse door, and pulled it shut after her—just in the nick of time!

A few moments later, she heard loud, angry voices, and they were coming closer. She recognized Mr. Bailey's voice. "This morning when I left, it was still there, and this afternoon when I came back, it was gone. There must have been burglars in the house sometime.

"I came to find out if your girl knows anything about it. She was at our place to do some cleaning today."

"I thought she was out here working in the garden this afternoon," Jacob said, "but she's not here now. I'll go and see if she's in the house."

Mary was coming out to the garden to see what the commotion was all about.

"Hello, Mrs. Yoder," Mr. Bailey greeted her. "I'd like to talk to Nancy. Where is she?"

"She was just here." Mary was puzzled. "Maybe she went over to the neighbors, the Fishers, just west of here. Why do you want to talk with Nancy?"

"A rare book was stolen out of my bookcase today." Mr. Bailey's voice was rising. "I wonder if she knows anything about it."

Jacob spoke up then, to the policeman. "I had a valuable book, a Bible, stolen out of my house, too, on Sunday. Maybe it was taken by the same thief that snitched Mr. Bailey's book."

The officer got out his notepad and began to

write down the information. He asked Jacob more questions. Meanwhile, Mr. Bailey shifted uneasily from one foot to the other.

My, he's impatient, thought Mary. *Why is he squirming like that?*

Before long Mr. Bailey broke in. "I forgot to mention to you that an antique dish was also stolen from my house. It was replaced by a cheap dish. And a seventeen-jewel watch disappeared, too."

The cop wrote all that down. Finally he looked up. "I'll see what I can do," he promised. "Where did you say this girl is that you want to question?"

Jacob spoke up. "We think she might be over at the neighbor's place. I'll go along over with you if you want to ask her questions."

Nancy was sitting there in the springhouse, beside the crocks of cream, shivering from fright and moaning softly. "*Ach, mei Zeit!* (oh, how awful). *Was soll ich duh* (what shall I do)?"

She covered her face with her hands and began to cry. After what seemed like a long time, Nancy again heard the sound of an auto in the drive. A car door slammed. Then she heard it leaving again.

"Naaancy, Naaancy," Jacob called. "Nancy, *wo bischt du* (where are you)?"

Nancy opened the springhouse door and went outside, blinking in the bright sunlight. It was no use hiding any longer. Mary and Jacob were standing on the porch, and Nancy sank down on the porch steps and sobbed out the whole story.

"We heard everything from Sally already," Mary told her. "Her dad got the truth out of her and made her give the Bible back to Mr. Bailey and confess what she did."

"Indeed, it was our Bible! The same records were in the front of it," reported Jacob. "But Mr. Bailey claimed he bought that Bible just last week. Since Sally had taken it out of Mr. Bailey's bookcase, and we had no way of proving it wasn't his, she had to give it back."

"Wh—what will they do with Sally and me?" Nancy wondered tearfully. "Will we be arrested or put in *die Bressent* (jail)?"

"No no," Jacob assured her. "I rather think the cop believed our story more than Mr. Bailey's, especially when Sally told him about your seeing Mr. Bailey's car in the lane on Sunday morning. But they have to have proof before they can do anything.

"So no charges will be pressed at this time. You and Sally were in the wrong by taking the Bible, though, but because of your age and the circumstances, nothing will be done."

Nancy, trembling, smiled through her tears. That sure was a load off her mind. "I'll never do such a dumb thing again!" she declared.

"I'm sure you won't," Jacob responded gently. "Now, I think you and Sally should write a letter of apology and send it to the Baileys right away."

"We will! We will!" Nancy promised.

26

Fantastic Plans

THAT evening at the supper table, Jacob explained that Amish people are *wehrlos* (defenseless, nonresistant). That was one reason why it was wrong for Nancy and Sally to take the Bible, even if they were sure it was stolen from them.

"I realize that now," Nancy admitted shamefacedly. "And I thought of that German verse that Mom drilled into us:

Klein Kind, lass sein
was nicht ist dein.

Child, leave alone
what you don't own.

"Well, I was sure the old Bible belonged to us, so I'd have a right to take it. But now I know better."

"We all keep learning as long as we live and have sound minds," Mary said kindly. "I remember when I was a *glee Meedel* (little girl) and *Maami un Daadi* (grandma and grandpa) Algyer were living yet. I once spent a week with them.

"Maami showed me a robin's nest in a bush, with four pretty blue eggs in it. Oh, how I longed to have those eggs. They seemed like rare and precious jewels to me.

"When Maami went to lie down for a nap in the afternoon, I climbed up and got the four eggs out of the nest and put them in my pocket. I played with them all the time that Maami was resting, and put them back in my pocket when she got up.

"After awhile I forgot about them and leaned against sink cabinet—and crunch! That was the end of the eggs. What a mess that was!

"Maami explained to me how cruel that was to poor Mr. and Mrs. Robin. That lesson I never forgot."

Jacob chuckled. "That reminds me of a story I once heard from the Great Depression days. A hungry man sneaked into his Amish neighbor's springhouse, helped himself to a pound of butter, and hid it under his hat.

"The farmer saw him come out and suspected what he had done. Pretending that nothing was amiss, he began to visit with the man.

"The thief tried to edge away, but the farmer just kept on talking to him and keeping him there. The sun was hot, and after awhile the butter began to melt and drip down the sides of the thief's face."

"You can't do wrong and get by," Mary said, "Sooner or later, everything will come out. The same goes for Mr. Bailey, whether he realizes it or not."

Jacob nodded. "It's not our place to bring him to justice. Sometimes we'd dearly like to get even with someone, but the Bible tells us that vengeance is the Lord's. God will straighten things out, in his own way. We're to return good for evil and to pray for those who use us badly."

Nancy knew that she deserved a lecture. Besides, she still felt guilty about that broken dish. What if it was worth thousands of dollars? And the wristwatch! Had Mrs. Bailey purposely given her that watch so she could say it was stolen?

Surely Mrs. Bailey wouldn't trap her like that! Maybe Mr. Bailey didn't know what happened to the watch. After supper she went out to the barn and felt around on the top of the barn beam where she had put the watch. It was nowhere to be found!

Nancy's heart sank. "Ach, it's enough to make a person cry," she groaned. "If only I wouldn't have accepted that watch! Now somebody has swiped it."

The barn door opened and Nancy heard voices. "Yahoo, where are you, Nancy?" somebody called.

"*Doh bin ich* (here I am)," Nancy replied.

It was the Fisher friends.

"Nancy, I'm so sorry I had to tell," Sally blurted out. "Now everything's spoiled! Ei yi yi! That Mr. Bailey has the nerve of a brass monkey!"

Nancy giggled at Sally's outburst. "I'm just glad they didn't put us in jail," she declared. "Taking that

Bible was a stupid thing for us to do."

"That sounds like one of Sally's scatterbrained ideas," Andrew muttered. "She has a habit of leaping before she looks."

"Now you're back to your teasing again," retorted Sally.

"It was my fault, too," Nancy admitted. "I wanted to get even with Mr. Bailey. But I know now that it wasn't right. Oh well, *so geht's* (so it goes). I guess that ends our cleaning job at the Baileys' place."

"Ya well, let's forget about it," Sally said. "We'll help you in the dairy barn. Then you can go for a spin in the pony spring wagon with us."

Nancy felt a surge of joy. It was good to have such loyal friends.

I won't worry about that wristwatch anymore, she thought. *Mrs. Bailey insisted on giving it to me, fair and square. It's not my fault it disappeared. I really didn't want to accept it in the first place.*

A short time later, the three piled on the pony spring wagon and were off. Andrew had just gotten rid of the sling. The doctor said his arm now was good for working, but not for racing or wrestling!

"Let's stop in at Barbie and Junior's and see what they're doing tonight," Sally suggested. "They usually have something going."

"Fine with me," Andrew agreed. "We can stay as long as we want to since I have this spring wagon wired for lights running off a battery." He reached down and turned a switch to show Nancy.

"*Wunderbaar!*" Nancy exclaimed. "Did you do it yourself?"

Andrew nodded, pleased at her praise. He reached down and pressed another switch. "Ooo-ga, ooo-ga," blared a horn.

Nancy jumped. "There's a car behind us, wanting to pass," she cried. "Pull over!"

Andrew and Sally burst out laughing. "That's just the horn we have here in the spring wagon."

Nancy blushed. "Next thing you'll be wanting to have a stereo installed yet, too."

"*Nee* (no), I'll never do that," Andrew protested. "I don't want to be one of the wild bunch like Aquila Riehl. Say, did you hear that he's having a singing and hoedown at his place on Sunday evening?"

"A hoedown?" Nancy quizzed. "You mean he's having a frolic to hoe the weeds in his fields?"

Andrew threw back his head and bellowed. "I said Sunday evening. We don't work on Sundays, you know."

"Stop bickering, you two," Sally scolded. "You both know that when they have a *Hop* (gathering) for the young people Sunday evenings, they sing first. Afterward, they have games and shenanigans, what they call a hoedown.

"Only Aquila's gang is invited, the wild bunch. I wouldn't mind being a mouse hiding somewhere and seeing what all goes on."

"Hey!" Andrew cried. "Why don't we?"

"Why don't we do what?" Sally asked. "Don't talk in riddles."

"Why don't we climb up into the *Hoibohre* (hay-mow) before the *Yunge* (young people) come? Then we can watch everything that goes on!"

"Do you mean it?" Sally gasped. "What if someone sees us?"

"Ach nee, it'll be dark up in the *Hoibohre*," Andrew assured them. "Aquila will probably hang a few gas lanterns on the *Riggel* (rails) in the barn, but we'll be way above that."

"We'd have to wait until everybody leaves to come down, and it might get awfully late," Sally reminded him.

"You mean awfully early," Andrew corrected her. "Early the next morning, I mean."

"I'm sure Mary and Jacob wouldn't let me be out so long," Nancy told them. "If I wouldn't be in by 9:00 or 9:30, Jacob would come looking for me."

"I just thought of something!" Sally exclaimed. "We could invite you over for the night. Then Mary and Jacob wouldn't know how late you're up."

"But what about your parents? Wouldn't they care if you're out way late?" Nancy wondered.

"They sure would!" For a few minutes Sally was stumped. But Andrew had another idea.

"We could all sleep outside in sleeping bags. Then Mom wouldn't know when we come in. Junior and Barbie probably want to be in on this, too. Junior and I could sleep in the barn, and you girls could sleep in the backyard under the pines."

"Oh, *ich bin so frehlich!* (I'm so glad)." Sally quivered with excitement. "I can hardly wait. I'm *gwunnerich* (curious) to know what a hoedown is like."

"Why is it called a hoedown?" Nancy wondered.

"I guess it's because they raise cane," Andrew joked. "We'll have to wait and see, though."

At the Bylers, Junior and Barbie were outside in the yard, trying out a new croquet set. Andrew guided the pony into the lane. Close to the barn, he tied him to the hitching ring on a post.

"Just who we need to help play croquet!" Junior called. "Come and each grab a mallet. We'll see who gets those balls through the wickets best."

"Just wait till you hear what we've planned for Sunday evening!" Andrew began. He told Junior and Barbie about their plans for having a slumber party and a hoedown watch.

Junior whistled a long, low whistle. "Do you really think we could do that without anyone seeing us go into the barn? What if we would be discovered?"

"We won't be discovered," Andrew declared. "We can hide in the cornfield behind the barn until it's nearly time for the first *Yunge* to arrive. Then we'll sneak up the ladder into the *Hoibohre*. Are you game to try it, or are you chicken?"

"*Wann du faddich bisht, ich bin aa* (if you're ready, I am too)," Junior replied.

"So am I," Barbie agreed. "I can hardly wait till next Sunday. That will be so exciting!"

That evening as Nancy lay in bed reliving the events of the day, she had a few misgivings. In her mind, one voice told her it would be best to make some excuse and drop out of the Sunday-night plans. But would they call her chicken? Another voice pulled her to be part of the fun.

Oh well, I don't have to decide right away, Nancy thought as she drifted off to sleep.

27

The Hoedown

THE week seemed long to Nancy because she and Mary were busy from dawn to dusk. There were bushels of peaches and baskets of tomatoes to can. But Sunday evening finally arrived.

Nancy had made up her mind that she would go with her friends to see what a hoedown was like. Mary and Jacob had given their permission for Nancy to sleep out, at the Fishers' place, and so everything was settled. Jacob had even loaned her his sleeping bag.

"Be sure you don't *gaxe* (cackle, chatter) and giggle more than you sleep," he teased. "And be certain you zip up the sleeping bag tightly so no *Schlang* (snake) can crawl in. I once heard of a boy that slept outside, and in the morning when he awoke, a snake was curled up in the sleeping bag with him."

"Jacob!" Mary scolded. "How you do *retze* (tease) Nancy! Next she won't be able to sleep a wink, with such thoughts on her mind."

"*Ach ya, es dutt mir leed* (oh yes, I'm sorry). I forgot how you hate snakes. Well, it's getting close to autumn now, and the snakes are likely slithering off for winter hibernation," Jacob consoled her.

"I don't think I'll lose sleep over snakes tonight," Nancy assured them.

She was feeling a bit guilty about what they were planning to do. *What would Mary and Jacob say if they knew?*

She promised, "I'll be home in time to help with the milking tomorrow morning, that is, if I don't *verschlofe mich* (oversleep)."

Then, with sleeping bag under her arm, she was on her way to the Fishers' place. Crickets were chirping in the mellow August evening, and a few late birds were twittering in the maple tree. The sun was sinking in the west, looking like a hazy red ball sending tranquil peace over the countryside.

"*Ach, ich kenn net waarde* (oh, I can't wait)." Nancy trembled with eager anticipation.

Yet, lurking in the back of her mind was that fear of being discovered. What would the *Yunge* do with them if they found them spying? Probably drag them down out of the *Hoibohre* and throw them over the fence. No way did they want such an embarrassing thing to happen!

On the Fishers' porch, Junior, Barbie, Andrew, and Sally were sitting on the rockers and glider, waiting for her.

"I'm so glad you could come," Sally called to her. "Come, Barbie, and I will show you where to put your sleeping bag. We're planning to sleep in Sarah's *Schpielhaus* (playhouse), that is, if we ever get to sleep.

"Mom and Dad thought it would get too damp to sleep outside. There'll be a heavy dew tonight."

"I'm glad we're sleeping inside," Nancy confessed. "Jacob was just teasing me about snakes crawling into sleeping bags!"

"Well, I'm certain no snakes can get into the *Schpielhaus*, even though it used to be a *Hinkelhaus* (chicken pen)," Sally said.

The *Schpielhaus* was surprisingly nice with a remnant of brown flowered carpet on the floor, nice feed sacks for curtains at each window, a homemade toy kitchen sink, a small wooden table and chairs, a child's rocker, a homemade dolly sofa, a high chair, and lots of *Lumbeboppe* (ragdolls).

"There's just enough room for us three here on the floor," Sally planned. "The boys will sleep in the barn. Mom and Dad are away visiting and will stay late. They'll never find out what time we come in."

"C'mon, it's time to be off!" Andrew was rattling the door. "We've got to be the first ones there."

"Have you heard any rigs go by yet?" Nancy asked.

"Rigs!" Andrew exclaimed. "You mean cars!" Don't you know that the wild bunch drives cars?"

"Ach, Andrew, not many of them," Sally retorted. "You know Aquila doesn't have a car."

"Well, he used to. They get rid of their cars when they join church and get married and are ready to settle down to be real Amish."

"Hurry up, let's go," Junior urged. "It's getting dark. If we're going to climb up into the haymow, I want to do it before the *Yunge* get there."

Nancy quivered with excitement as they sneaked into the cornfield and headed for Aquila's barn.

"Bend over to walk so you won't get all *schtruwwlich* (hair messed up)," Sally told the girls. "The cornstalk leaves make me feel all *beissich* (itchy), too, if I don't bend over."

"Psch! (shhh)," Andrew warned. "We don't want anyone to hear us."

An owl hooted from a tree in the fencerow, and somewhere a dog was howling dismally.

"Does Aquila have a dog?" Nancy whispered.

"Not loose," Sally whispered back. "He has his dogs penned up, like Jacob does with his purebred dogs."

"I hope we don't get lost," Barbie said anxiously. "Everything looks the same in here."

"Follow the leader," Andrew told her. "I'm staying in this fourth row, so we can't lose our way."

Finally they were at the end of the field.

"Now wait here," Andrew whispered, "while I sneak up to the little door on the barn hill and peek inside to see if the coast is clear."

A moment later he was motioning them to join him. On the barn floor, it was darker, but they knew their way from playing *Blummesack* (bag tag) there.

"*Nuff die Leeder, eens uff amol* (up the ladder, one at a time)," he commanded. "Hurry, but *geb acht* (take care) that you don't fall."

"Why don't we all go up at once?" Barbie asked. "This makes me nervous, standing here waiting."

Andrew replied, "Because if we'd all be on the ladder at once, and the top one would fall, we would all *schtatze hie* (fall down). Then we'd be like the preachers I heard about.

"One Sunday they were returning from the *Abrot* (council meeting). Coming downstairs, the last one at the top of the steps tripped and hit the second in line, who fell forward and hit the next one, and so on, down to the bottom one.

"The people were surprised when the stair door burst open. All the preachers came flying out and landed on a pile. The church almost quit singing."

"Andrew Fisher!" Sally hissed. "How disrespectful can you get? Making fun of the preachers like that! You know that story isn't true!"

"Calm down, sis. I didn't make up that story. Now *drummel dich* (hurry)! It's your turn to go up the ladder."

"Well, it's rude for you to even repeat such a story," Sally scolded.

Nancy was the last one up. When nearly at the top, she heard someone coming into the barn.

"*Mach schnell,* Nancy," Barbie whispered. "It's Aquila coming with the lanterns."

Nancy shuddered. What if she shook so badly that she fell down? But she was near the top, and Sally reached out and pulled her to safety.

"Now be quieter than a mouse," Andrew whispered. "That was close. We made it just in the nick of time. Lie flat on your stomachs."

They lay there in a row, peeping over the edge of the mow to see Aquila.

Aquila left after he set the lanterns, and all was quiet for awhile.

Sally yawned. "If I fall asleep, wake me up. But not Andrew, please. He might play a trick on me like he did on Junior at church."

"*Psch!*" Andrew muttered. "Can't you forget that once?"

"Hey, what's that noise?" Barbie asked fearfully. "It sounded close."

"It's just the pigeons flying into the barn to roost," Andrew told her. "That's the whirring of their wings. Say, why didn't we bring our sacks? We have our flashlights, and we could get the rest of the pigeons while we wait."

"*Sei schtill!* (be quiet). Somebody's coming," Sally whispered.

It was a group of girls, chattering merrily. *My, they dress for fancy,* Nancy thought. *They're either crowding the fence of the Ordnung (church rules) or not obeying them at all. But I guess they're not church members yet.*

By the light of the flickering gas lanterns, they watched from the shadowy haymow as more and more *Yunge* came into the barn. Soon they began to sing church songs, even though many of the boys had not come in yet.

When the singing was over and the party games began, the rest of the boys came in. They brought different music with them. The barn was filled with a rhythmic beat and the thumping of many feet on the barn floor.

The group in the haymow, lying on their stomachs and peering down at the goings-on below, watched in fascination at first. But after awhile they grew more and more drowsy.

"Ho hum, I'm *schleeferich.* I wish I'd be at home in bed," Andrew grumbled. "This is just more and more of the same thing. They're just *schtambing* (stamping) around. And now we can't even get out until they all leave. Disgusting!"

Nancy had been up early to help with the milking, and she felt herself getting more and more *schleeferich,* too. She tried to prop her eyelids open with her fingers, but that didn't do a bit of good. Finally she gave up and let herself doze off. Before long, all of them in the haymow were fast asleep.

28

Shadow and Sun

NANCY awakened with a start. Somebody was yelling. She rubbed her eyes sleepily and blinked.

Where am I? she wondered. Then it dawned on her. She was still in the haymow in Aquila's barn.

"What's going on?" a sleepy voice asked. It was Sally.

"*Psch!*" Nancy warned. "They'll hear you."

More shouts were heard from the floor below.

"*Was in die Welt* (what in the world)?" Andrew exclaimed, just waking up, too. "What's going on down there?"

They all peered down to the barn floor. Most of the *Yunge* had cleared out, and only a few stragglers remained.

"It looks like someone is picking a fight," Junior whispered. "They sound as mad as hornets."

"Fists are flying," Barbie moaned. "Oooh, I can't bear to watch."

"It's Aquila and another guy," Andrew observed. "Aquila's acting like a banty *Haahne* (rooster). He's warning the other fellow to stay away from his girl."

"Maybe they're just wrestling to see who's the strongest," Nancy said hopefully.

"Hmph!" Andrew snorted. "Like fun! They're really after each other!"

Aquila drew back and aimed with his fist. He struck just as the other guy lunged forward, and Aquila's fist hit him on the neck. He fell to the floor limply and lay still.

"He's killed! He's dead!" Barbie cried wildly, forgetting to be quiet.

The shocked group below took no notice of her. Someone ran for the phone shanty to call an ambulance.

"Let's go down. I can't bear to stay up here any longer," Andrew declared. None of them needed a second invitation.

Nancy was trembling again. "Ach my," she moaned. "I hope I'm not shaking so much that I can't climb down." But finally she reached the barn floor.

"Whoever the guy is, he's not dead," Sally observed. "See, they're talking to him."

"Maybe he's paralyzed," Junior said sadly. "Why else wouldn't he get up or move even just a bit?"

Aquila was pacing the floor and wringing his

hands. The *Yunge* were too upset to notice the youngsters from the haymow.

"Let's go home," Andrew said. "We can't do a thing to help anyway."

It was a sad and frightened group that trudged homeward. The wail of an ambulance siren could be heard in the distance, getting closer.

Nancy was shivering. "I'm going home to Mary and Jacob," she said in a small voice. "I couldn't sleep a wink anyway."

"I'm going home, too," Barbie said.

Clouds were scudding in front of the moon, and several dogs in the neighborhood were howling eerily in tune with the siren.

"Shall we walk home with you?" Sally asked Nancy.

"No. It's not far. I'll run the rest of the way."

At Mary and Jacob's house, the kitchen door was left unlocked for her, and Nancy crept inside.

"I think I'll wake them up," Nancy decided. "I have to talk to someone about this."

She struck a match and lit the kerosene lamp that Mary had put on the kitchen table. It was not as bright as the gas lamps that usually lighted the kitchen, and it cast flickering shadows on the walls.

Nancy knocked softly on the door of the downstairs bedroom, where Mary and Jacob slept, but there was no response. She knocked louder and waited. Still no response!

My, they must be sound sleepers, she thought. She rapped sharply, waiting to hear them stirring and answering, but all was quiet. What a lonely, desolate feeling she had! Should she bang loudly on the door, or let them sleep on?

Nancy paced the floor, wondering what to do. Suddenly a piece of paper on the table caught her attention. A note! Why hadn't she seen it before? She quickly read it.

Dear Nancy,

We had to leave for the hospital at midnight. So it was good you were at the Fishers overnight.

I'll try to be back for the morning milking. If I'm late, let the cows in and do what you usually do, until I come.

Jacob

Nancy gasped. They were at the hospital! She wondered why. Then it dawned on her that she was all alone in the house, and she felt frightened. Should she run back to Sally? No, maybe Sally was in her bed and had locked the door.

With a whimper, Nancy threw herself on the couch and covered herself with the afghan. Still she was trembling.

"Oh, I wish morning were here," she muttered.

Every now and then the house creaked, and she shuddered with fear. Then she realized how childish she was acting.

"Nancy Petersheim!" she scolded herself. "You must be brave and stop acting like a baby."

She willed herself to calm down and relax. Gradually she quieted down enough to drop off to sleep. When she awoke, the sun was streaming in through the kitchen window, and Jacob was standing there smiling at her.

"Hello, Aunt Nancy," he teased.

"What?" Nancy asked, blinking her eyes and trying to rub the sleep from them.

"You're an aunt now!"

It took awhile for it to enter Nancy's mind. She sat there, blinking. "An aunt?"

"Yes, you have a little niece."

Then it sank in, and her eyes lit up in glad surprise. "A *Buppeli?* Mary has a *Buppeli?*"

"Yes, a tiny little girl. She's early, and they call her a preemie. So she'll have to stay at the hospital several weeks. We thought she wouldn't come till after you were back in school, but we sure can use your help now."

Nancy jumped up. She realized that keeping house for Jacob was on her shoulders until Mary came home. And it was time to begin the chores.

After she was in the milk house putting together the milkers, the memories of the last evening came back to her, and some of her happiness drained away.

I'll have to tell Jacob all about it, she decided. *It's no use putting it off until later.*

While they were feeding the cows, Nancy summoned the courage to tell Jacob all that had happened.

His eyes were grave as he responded, "It's my duty to take care of my wife's little sister while she's living under our roof. If I'd known you were planning such pranks, I'd certainly not have let you go."

Nancy hung her head. "I'm sorry," she murmured. "I realize now that I shouldn't have gone."

"How badly was the fellow hurt?" Jacob asked.

"I don't know," Nancy said. "Junior thought he looked like he was paralyzed. But we left before the emergency medical people got there."

Jacob shook his head in sympathy. "I sure hope it's not as serious as it sounds. But maybe there's a lesson in it for us all. Sometimes such things are the only way God can speak to us." He went back to feeding the cows.

Nancy hurried to finish her chores. Monday was washday, and she would have to carry on without Mary. Jacob helped her fill the big furnace kettle with water and made a fire underneath to heat the wash water.

"Tell me when the water is boiling, and I'll dip it into the washing machine for you," Jacob told her. "I don't want you to do that and run the risk of scalding yourself. Boiling water is dangerous. I'll start the washer engine for you then, too."

Nancy was grateful for Jacob's help, and also that it was a sunny, breezy day for drying the laundry. By suppertime all the clothes were dried, folded, and put back in place except for Jacob's white shirt and the Sunday dresses, which would have to be ironed.

After the milking was finished, Sally came over.

"Have you heard anything about the injured boy?" Nancy wondered.

"No, I haven't," Sally replied. "But I did hear that Aquila is taking it really hard. He didn't mean to cause so much injury. Now he's sorry for what he did and blames himself. Poor Aquila! Maybe this will help him to truly repent and become a sincere Christian. If so, maybe some good will come of the fight."

Jacob came in from the barn. "Have you told Sally the good news?" he asked.

"Not yet, but I was just going to," Nancy said. "Mary and Jacob have a little girl baby!"

"Honest?" Sally said in amazement. "What's her name?"

Nancy clapped her hands to her mouth. "I was so excited about it that I forgot to ask. Does she have a name already?" she asked Jacob.

Jacob chuckled. "It tickled me so that you forgot to ask. I was just waiting to see how long it would go until you would think of it. Her name is Nancy Ann, named after you!"

Nancy's eyes shone. What an honor that was!

"Oh Nancy, you're so *glicklich* (lucky)!" Sally exclaimed. "That makes me jealous. It's not fair that I won't have a niece for years and years yet. But I guess that's just the way life is."

It surely is! Nancy thought. *A mixture of shadow and sun*.

29

Mary's Mistake

HAVING a preemie in the hospital meant that bills were mounting every day. There was no way Jacob could pay them himself. By Amish custom, he had no insurance. But he could depend on the church people to help pay the bill. Many men quietly made donations through the deacon.

To raise more money, some of the women got together, made over a thousand subs, and sold them at an auction sale. Others made quilt tops and put them in frames. Then the church women got together and quilted them. They would be sold to tourists.

Other women organized a bake sale at some local farm auctions. They brought many shoofly pies, fruit pies, doughnuts, cakes, cookies, and whoopie pies to sell. All the proceeds from these projects went to help pay hospital bills for Mary and little Nancy Ann.

Nancy was extra busy until Mary came home after two days in the hospital. Then there was a little less on her shoulders. Church people were helping with dinner that first week. They took turns bringing a main dish and a dessert for the family every noon, as they had done when Mary's leg was hurt. Usually the leftovers helped with supper.

The community was greatly relieved to hear that the boy injured in Aquila's barn was not paralyzed after all. He had three cracked vertebrae and had to wear a neck brace until they were healed.

There was hardly a soul more grateful than Aquila himself.

"He's a different person, they tell me," Jacob reported at the supper table one evening. "He's meek and repentant, and he has made things right with Deacon Miller and the church. He has confessed to the ministers his earlier deception and is doing all he can to make amends."

"*Ich bin so froh* (I'm so glad) that he repented and now is going to become a faithful member of the church," Mary commented warmly. "God surely does move in a mysterious way to perform his wonders."

"Say, Nancy," Jacob proposed, "would you like to go along to the hospital tonight to visit baby Nancy Ann? You haven't seen her yet. I'm going to the phone shanty now to call Mrs. Davis to see if it will suit her to take Mary to the hospital.

"I've been going in every evening, and tonight I should grind feed. So I'm giving you the chance to go along."

"Would I!" Nancy cried, her eyes shining. "I'm so eager to see the baby, and I've never visited anyone at the hospital before."

Mary was peering out the window. "There's a car coming in the lane now. Who might that be?"

"Why, it's Mrs. Bailey!" Nancy gasped. A stab of fear shot through her. Was she still going to confront Nancy about the broken dish?

However, Mrs. Bailey had something much more important on her mind. She came to the door, leaning heavily on her cane and looking sad. "Did you hear that my husband is in the hospital?"

"No, we didn't. What happened?" Jacob responded with concern.

"I—I think he had a heart attack." Mrs. Bailey wiped away a tear. "He's in intensive care."

"That's too bad!" Mary's voice showed feeling. "I hope he'll have a complete and speedy recovery."

"Thank you! I guess time will tell." Mrs. Bailey's face was creased with care. "I heard that you people have a baby in the hospital and wondered if anyone would like to ride along there with me tonight?"

"Why, yes, we're glad for the chance," Mary told her. "How thoughtful of you to remember us in the midst of your own troubles."

"I guess I'm feeling lonely," Mrs. Bailey admitted. "Now just take your time getting ready. I'll wait in the car."

"I'll be needing some money," Mary told Jacob,

"to pay Mrs. Bailey for the ride."

Jacob looked worried. "Money is getting to be as scarce as hen's teeth. But here's a twenty-dollar bill. It's the last I have, so take good care of it."

"I will," Mary promised. "I feel guilty that you bought me that secretary's desk."

"Well, we can always sell it again, if we really have to," Jacob replied. "I didn't know then that we'd have so many hospital bills."

Ten minutes later, they were in Mrs. Bailey's car, Mary in front with Mrs. Bailey, and Nancy in back.

At least she's not holding a grudge against me, Nancy thought. *She's chatting pleasantly with Mary.*

As they hit the highway, she marveled, *My, a car goes fast, just like a whir. And then the scenery is past. No chance to hear the birds.*

When they stopped at a crossing, two cars were coming from the left, but Mrs. Bailey pulled out anyway. Nancy quickly stifled a scream, but they made it across easily before the cars were too close.

Whew! We'd never have made it with the horse! These fast cars can do just about anything. But the traffic makes me nervous.

Soon they were in the city. *What a lot of buildings and people!* When Nancy saw a little African-American girl walking with her mother on the sidewalk, she thought of Lakisha.

Nancy stared in awe when they pulled in at the hospital entrance. So many stories stacked on top of each other! She wondered what floor little Nancy Ann was on.

"I'll drop you off here at the lobby," Mrs. Bailey

told them. "After the visiting hours are over, I'll meet you here again and show you where I've parked the car."

Mary and Sally got out and entered the building.

"Have you ever been on an elevator?" Mary asked.

Nancy shook her head.

"Well, we're going up in one now."

Mary pressed a button, a door slid open, and they stepped into a little room. When they began to go up, Nancy felt a sinking feeling in the pit of her stomach and grabbed Mary's arm.

Mary chuckled. "You'll get used to it soon," she assured Nancy. "We'll be there in no time at all."

And so it was. In a few seconds, they were stepping into the hall, on solid footing again.

"Do you think I'll be allowed to hold the baby?" Nancy asked wistfully as they walked the hall.

"No, I'm afraid you won't even be allowed in the same room with her. I'm sorry about it, but that's in the hospital rules. I'll bring her to the window so you can see her, though."

Before holding the baby, Mary had to wash her hands and don a hospital gown. In a few minutes she brought the tiny bundle to the window.

Nancy stared, entranced. The baby had lots of dark brown hair, such tiny little fists, and a wee little nose. She was much smaller than baby Lydia had been when she was born.

"Isn't she a dearie?" came from a voice at Nancy's elbow. An elderly, pleasant-looking African-American woman stood there, admiring the baby, too. "Is she your sister?"

"No, my niece. But she's named after me—Nancy Ann."

"Well, I had a little preemie grandbaby a few years ago, and he was a lot smaller than your baby is. He only weighed two and a half pounds."

The friendly woman kept on visiting with Nancy in the lounge. When Mary came back out, she struck up a friendly conversation with her, too.

"My, what a sweet baby you have. And she's not nearly as tiny as my grandson down in Texas was. He was in the hospital for eight weeks. How long will your baby have to stay?"

"The doctor thinks in three or four weeks she can come home. She's doing quite well so far, and they say she's started to gain."

"Well, praise the Lord! My grandson has cerebral palsy, and he didn't do so well. He still has a lot of problems. Will you pray for him?"

"Yes, we'll do that," Mary promised.

The woman smiled her thanks. "And I'll pray for your baby, too, that she'll continue doing well." She got up to leave.

"Do you want to go to the rest room before we leave?" Mary asked Nancy. "You might as well."

Nancy nodded.

"I think I'll go, too," the black lady said.

In the rest room, Nancy held Mary's purse until Mary came out of the stall. By then the lady had gone.

While Nancy was in the stall, Mary pulled a handkerchief out of her purse. Suddenly she thought, *Ja-*

cob told me to take care of that twenty dollars. She quickly checked to see if the bill was still there. It was not on top like it had been!

Mary searched frantically in her purse but couldn't find it anywhere. With a sinking heart, Mary decided that it was gone.

Finally she looked around the floor, and sure enough, there under the sink lay the twenty-dollar bill! Mary quickly snatched it and put it back in her purse.

When Mary and Nancy came out of the rest room, they caught up to the black lady near the elevator, rummaging in her own purse as though she had lost something. She looked up and said, "Well, good-bye. It was so nice talking to you. God bless you!"

"Good-bye, and thank you," Mary responded.

A few minutes later, Mary and Nancy joined Mrs. Bailey in the lobby. "Ready to go?" she asked. "My car is parked not far from here."

As they walked to the car, she added, "Well, I feel a lot happier than I did when I came. I'll tell you why on the way home."

She guided the car through the traffic and shared about her husband. "He's a lot better and out of the intensive care unit. It wasn't his heart after all. The doctor thinks it was probably a stomach ulcer, which isn't nearly as serious."

"That's sure good news," Mary rejoiced with her. "Can he come home soon?"

"Yes. They're only going to do a few tests first. If everything else shows clear, they'll give him medication and send him home."

The trip home didn't seem long, and in a short time they were pulling in the Yoders' lane. "What do I owe you for the trip?" Mary asked Mrs. Bailey.

Mrs. Bailey shook her head. "Not a cent. I was going that way anyway."

"Well, thanks so much!" Mary was relieved, thinking how pleased Jacob would be to have his twenty dollars back. "I'll send you a loaf of homemade bread sometime," she promised. "Or maybe a pie."

"I won't refuse that!" Mrs. Bailey laughed. "I know you're a good cook.

"And Nancy, thanks for that letter you and Sally sent us. We sure don't hold anything against you. It was a misunderstanding, and I admire your courage for apologizing."

"Well, thanks, Mrs. Bailey," Nancy murmured sheepishly.

Jacob was waiting up for Mary and Nancy in the kitchen. "How was Nancy Ann?" he wondered first thing.

"Doing great, according to the nurses," Mary replied. "I think I even got a smile out of her tonight. But it might have been only the result of a bit of bellyache.

"And Mr. Bailey is much better, too. Mrs. Bailey didn't accept any money for the trip. But you'd never guess what almost happened to your twenty-dollar bill." She grinned. "If I hadn't done some quick searching, you'd never have seen it again."

She opened her purse and got out the twenty-dollar bill. Then she gasped. Hidden under an envelope, with only a corner of it showing, was *another* twenty-dollar bill!

Mary groaned, sat down in a chair, and covered her face with her hands. "Ach, mei, I could cry," she moaned. "I think I stole that nice lady's twenty dollars!

"Ach, was soll ich duh (oh, what shall I do)? What will she think of me? She'll likely expect all Amish people to be thieves."

Mary could hardly get over it.

"What does she mean?" Jacob asked Nancy, looking bewildered. But Nancy was just as mystified.

When Mary explained what had happened, Jacob and Nancy agreed that the extra twenty-dollar bill had likely been dropped by the lady they met at the hospital.

"We need to try to give it back," Jacob said soberly. "I'll go to the phone shanty tomorrow and talk with one of the nurses. Maybe someone knows the black woman or can find out her name."

Mary kept blaming herself. "Here I was explaining to Nancy why it was wrong to steal back the Froschauer Bible. Now I feel like an utter failure."

"Well, you certainly didn't mean to steal," Jacob reassured her. "It was lost, and you found it. Now we'll try to find the woman. But whether we can or can't, I think it's best for you to forgive yourself."

But Mary would not be comforted. "I just hope I'll never forget the lesson I learned tonight. I'll rue my mistake till the day I die."

30

Confessions

ANOTHER week passed with Mary going to the hospital every day. Jacob and Nancy took turns going with her.

No one could identify the black woman whose twenty dollars Mary had found. Mary wept bitterly. But what was done, was done.

On Friday evening as they sat at the supper table, they heard a knock at the door.

"It's Mr. Bailey," Nancy said in dismay when she saw him through the screen door.

"Come right in," Jacob called out loudly. "You're just in time for supper."

"Thanks, but I'm not staying long." Mr. Bailey stepped inside.

"Nancy, will you pull out a chair for him?" Mary asked. "He was just in the hospital."

"Thank you," Mr. Bailey responded as he lowered himself into the chair gingerly. "I'm still having some stomach pain, but otherwise I'm all right. The doctor has me drinking goat's milk to help the ulcer heal. I had to ask around and finally found some at a farm about five miles away."

"Maybe we should get a goat for Nancy to milk," Jacob suggested. "Then you could get milk from us."

"Well, I'm not here just to talk. I came to return your Froschauer Bible." He walked over to the table and handed Jacob a heavy, wrapped package.

Jacob blinked in surprise. "You—you don't mean . . . you didn't. . . ."

"I did!" Mr. Bailey replied grimly. "One Sunday when you were in church, I took it. I had offered four-hundred dollars for the Bible, and when you declined, I helped myself.

"I told myself it wasn't stealing because I put five hundred-dollar bills under the shelf clock in the sitting room. I told myself it was all right, because I gave a hundred more than we'd been talking about. But now I've come to make things right."

Mary gasped. "You mean the five hundred dollars is still there?"

"I suppose so, if nobody found it," Mr. Bailey said.

Jacob got up, went into the *Sitzschtupp*, and returned with the five hundred-dollar bills. He looked completely flabbergasted.

Mr. Bailey went on, "When I was lying flat on my

back in intensive care, not knowing whether I'd live to see another day, I knew I wanted to make things right with you. So here's the Bible."

Jacob spoke up, "If you'd like to have the Bible that much, why don't we leave things as they are? I'm badly in need of money just now, with all these hospital bills, and this five hundred will come in handy."

"I'd really like to have the Bible," Mr. Bailey admitted. "But I have something else to confess. That Bible is really rare. It's worth a lot more than five hundred. If you're interested, we could take it to the historical society and have it appraised. I'll pay you whatever they say it's worth."

"That's fine with me," Jacob agreed happily. "But I feel almost guilty for accepting a lot of money for it."

"Don't feel guilty. I know you're a struggling young farmer, and I have plenty enough money laid up to last me and my wife the rest of our lives, and more. Insurance takes care of our hospital bills. I'm sorry for what I did, and I want to make it right."

"Well, you surely are doing that," Jacob told him. "Here, I'll give you your money back until we come to another agreement."

"No, you just keep that," Mr. Bailey insisted. "Consider that as a down payment." He shook hands with Jacob, then walked to the door.

Nancy cleared her throat. All the while the men had been talking, she was trying to summon up enough courage to confess about the broken dish. It was now or never!

"Mr. Bailey," she piped up in a weak and frightened tone. "I accidentally broke your antique dish when I was dusting, so I buried the pieces under the spruce trees. I replaced it with a dish Mary let me have. But I should have told you right away."

Mr. Bailey looked puzzled at first, then the light dawned on his face. He threw back his head and laughed. "So that's what happened. Well, don't worry about it. That dish wasn't worth more than ten or fifteen dollars.

"You can come over and do a few hours of cleaning for my wife to make up for it, if that will make you feel better."

That was a big load off Nancy's shoulders! She felt so relieved and almost light-headed.

"Oh, another thing," Mr. Bailey added. "I found my wristwatch behind the dresser. One of us must've knocked it down without realizing it. So it wasn't stolen after all."

"You mean the watch Mrs. Bailey gave me wasn't the valuable one?" Nancy asked.

"Oh no, no!" Mr. Bailey assured her. "That one is yours to keep, no matter what its worth. She gave that to you as a gift."

"Thank you!" Nancy's eyes were shining with gratefulness. That was another load off her mind.

After Mr. Bailey left, Mary quizzed her. "What watch were you talking about?"

So Nancy explained to Mary and Jacob that Mrs. Bailey gave her the watch, she hid it in the barn, and it later disappeared.

"Well now, that *is* a puzzle," Jacob declared. "Another riddle to solve. But it's nothing really important."

That evening as Nancy helped to feed the calves and carry milk, she felt more lighthearted than she had for a long time.

If something is bothering me and making me feel guilty, I'll never again let it go unsettled, she decided. *I feel so much better when I confess it and get it off my mind. The longer I let it go, the harder it is to do it.*

She stood at the west barn door, watching the sunset, a maze of crimson and gold with broken clouds mixed throughout. Her gaze reached down into the meadow, to a row of birches by the creek. Their leaves quivered in the evening breeze; now and then a leaf fell into the water and drifted downstream.

My summer vacation will soon be over, Nancy mused, *and I'll be back at Whispering Brook Farm. It was a good summer. I made new friends and had a lot of experience here in keeping house.*

With the burden of blunders off her back, she felt so free to enjoy the colors changing as the sun was setting. Suddenly she realized that she had learned more than one kind of housekeeping that summer.

Taking care of mistakes right away is just good housekeeping with my family and friends, she told herself. *It's good inner housekeeping, too.*

Now I'm ready to go back to Whispering Brook Farm. I just hope little Nancy Ann will come home from the hospital before I have to go home.

The barn door opened, and Sally came in. "Guess what I have for you," she said to Nancy. But she couldn't wait for Nancy to make a guess. "A letter from Lakisha! Here, read it! She wants me and you to be her pen pals."

Nancy took the letter and read it eagerly.

"Why don't we start a circle letter?" she suggested. "Tyler and Andrew and Junior could be in it, too."

"I've heard of a circle letter," Sally responded, "but I'm not sure how it works. Tell me about it."

So Nancy explained, "Mom's in a circle letter with her brothers and sisters. They just keep sending the pack of letters to each other, and every time it comes around, you put a new letter in and take your old one out."

"That sounds interesting. I'll ask Andrew if he wants to join. I hope he's not too *grossfielich* (big feeling) to be in a circle letter with girls. Why don't you ask him yourself the next time he comes over? He wouldn't have the nerve to turn you down."

Nancy giggled. "I don't want anyone to feel forced. It's just for whoever wants to join."

"I think he'll be interested though, if you're in it," Sally surmised. "He thinks a lot of you."

"*Schtobb mich retze* (stop teasing me), Sally!" Nancy scolded, giving Sally a playful pinch.

Sally put her hands on her hips. "*Schtobb mich petze!* (stop pinching me), Nancy." She pretended to be angry.

Both girls began to giggle helplessly.

"We're starting to speak in poetry," gasped Nancy.

"Oh, Nancy, I'm going to miss you *wunderbaar*

when you go home," Sally confided.

"That's why I want you to write to me," Nancy told her, "so I don't get so *Heemweh* for you."

"I will," Sally promised. "But now I've got to go and help Mom make a dress for Sarah."

Nancy and Sally waved to each other until Sally disappeared around the curve in the road. Nancy walked slowly back to the milk house.

Life is full of partings, she mused a bit sadly. *But so geht's (so it goes). We'll have letters and next summer.*

31

Homecoming

NANCY was filled with excitement. It was the last week of August. A lot of good things were happening today.

First, baby Nancy Ann was coming home from the hospital. Second, the whole family was coming in a van to see the new arrival—Mom, Dad, Joe, Omar, Steven, Henry, Susie, Lydia, and even Mammi.

Then Nancy was going along home with them so she'd be there when school started. Six-year-old Susie was not going to school yet, so she would stay, to be a *Kindmaut* (child helper) for Mary.

Nancy was hurrying around, wanting to get everything spick-and-span.

"It wonders me who will get here first—Mary and

Jacob, home from the hospital? Or the van with my family?" Nancy spoke aloud, talking to keep company with herself. "I just wish Nancy Ann could have come home before my last day here."

Just then, to Nancy's surprise, the door opened, and in walked Mom and Dad and the rest of the family.

"What?" Nancy was astonished. "I didn't see you driving in."

"Well, we're here!" Dad greeted her cheerily.

Susie and Lydia hugged Nancy, and Mom did an unusual thing: she kissed Nancy lovingly on the cheek. Mammi shook hands with her.

Suddenly, with these greetings, Nancy realized how much she had missed them all.

"My, you have really grown this summer," Maami told her. "Our little Nancy has disappeared, and a tall, grown-up Nancy has taken her place."

Joe tweaked her ear. "Next thing you'll be ready for *rumschpringing* (running around with the young people)."

Nancy's face was flushed with excitement. It was so good to see them all again!

Omar, standing by the window, reported, "Mary and Jacob are home!"

Everyone went out to the yard to meet them. Nancy was relieved not to be the center of attention anymore. Now they all were cooing over Nancy Ann, and the oohs and aahs were for her.

"*Ich will sie hewe* (I want to hold her)," Susie cried right away. Mary told her to sit on the couch and put the baby in her arms.

The whole family crowded around to admire her. It was Mom and Dad's first *Kinskind* (grandchild) and the children's first niece. And now Maami was a *Gross-grossmammi* (great-grandmother).

"She has your eyes and mouth, Mary," Mom decided, "and Jacob's chin and hairline."

Mary laughed. "I was thinking all the time that she looks a bit like you, Mamm. Just the shape of her nose, or her dimples. And her eyebrows are shaped like Daed's."

Dad chuckled. "I guess she looks just like herself. A very nice baby she is."

Mary gave the baby to Nancy to cuddle for a few minutes.

"Oh, I love you so, Nancy Ann!" Nancy whispered.

Jacob asked the new grandparents, "Can you believe that you're a Mammi and Daadi now?"

"I guess we'll have to," Mom replied, "but I don't know if we're wise enough yet to live up to that."

"Look!" Steven cried. "She has a cowlick in her hair! That means she'll be smart."

The baby slept peacefully, unaware that she was being inspected. Mary took her from Nancy and gently laid her in the cradle.

"Well, Nancy, you'll have to tell us what to do," Mom said. "We want to help you with the work. Shall I peel potatoes for dinner?"

"Yes. I'll peel potatoes, too, and I want you to make the stuffing," Nancy told her. "There's a big chicken roasting in the oven. And could you make the gravy, too, so it doesn't turn lumpy?"

"I'll help, too," the new great-grandmother offered. "I'll peel the peaches."

The menfolk went into the *Sitzschtupp* to visit until dinner was ready. The Froschauer Bible lay on top of the secretary desk. Dad looked at it carefully, and Jacob told them the whole story of what had happened to it and how he got it back. He even briefly mentioned the broken dish and the missing watch.

"That story is almost unbelievable," Dad responded. "But I think it fits with what Steven and Henry have to say about a watch."

Steven pulled the wristwatch out of his pocket and showed it to Jacob. "I found this on a beam in your barn the last time we were here. We knew it wasn't yours and guessed that it was left there by the previous farmer."

Jacob took the watch. "I'll ask Nancy if this is the one the Mrs. Bailey gave her."

Nancy was grating *Graut* (cabbage) for slaw. "Come here a minute," Jacob called. "Is this the watch you had?"

Nancy's eyes lit up. "Yes, that's the one. Where did you find it?"

"Steven found it right where you had put it and took it along home. Now he brought it back."

Nancy knew she would not be allowed to wear the watch and did some quick thinking. "If it's all right, I'd like to send this watch to Lakisha, the Fresh Air girl, in New York City. I know she'd be really glad for it."

"That's a good idea," Jacob approved.

So it was agreed that the watch should be sent to Lakisha.

"Come, dinner is ready," Mom called to the men and boys a short time later.

The family needed no second invitation, and all gathered at the table.

"*Mir welle bitte um Sege* (we want to ask the blessing)," Jacob said, and all bowed their heads in silent prayer.

Nancy's heart was filled to overflowing with thankfulness. Once more the whole family was together. No one was missing, . . . except Daadi, of course, who was in a better place.

How I wish it could always stay this way, and we could always be together like this, Nancy thought. But in her heart she knew it couldn't always be so. One by one they would get married and leave, and the family would be scattered. Such is life!

But then there would be more *schnuck Buppelin* (cute babies) to hold, and Nancy's heart was cheered at that prospect.

With Mom's expert help, the *Middaagesse* (dinner) had turned out just right. The chicken was roasted crisp and golden, the mashed potatoes were light and fluffy and drizzled with browned homemade butter, and the stuffing with gravy and giblets was done to perfection. There were steaming ears of corn on the cob, slices of ripe red tomatoes, and creamy cabbage slaw.

For dessert Mom had brought blueberry pies and chocolate whoopie pies, and they had the fresh peaches that Mammi had peeled.

"Nancy must be a *gute Koch* (good cook)," Joe complimented.

"She is," Jacob confirmed. "However, Mamm and Mammi probably get some of the credit for this meal."

Nancy blushed at the praise, which she felt was undeserved. What would they think if they knew she had burned the *Gnepplin* (dumplings) and buried them?

"Yes, I believe you learned a lot this summer, didn't you?" Mary asked.

"In more ways than one—not just in cooking," Nancy agreed. "But I still have a lot to learn. I just wish that baby Nancy Ann would have come home sooner. It spites me that I have to leave on the very day she came home."

"*Ya well, so geht's,*" Mom said. "We're having a barn raising next month to add a wing to the barn. Maybe Mary and Jacob and baby Nancy can come for the day. That would give you a chance to hold her to your heart's content."

"Me too," Susie piped up. "I'll come along, too."

"So you will," Mom assured her.

The rest of the day passed quickly. Mom and the girls made noodle dough and put it through Mary's noodle maker. Then they hung the flat sheets of dough up to dry. Later they put them through the noodle cutter, slicing them into thin strips. The homemade noodles were so much better than the store-bought ones.

Baby Nancy Ann slept the afternoon away, peaceful and undisturbed, much to the little girls' disappointment. At four o'clock Henry came running into the kitchen. "The van's here," he called. "Get ready to start for home."

As the family got into the van, Nancy felt the pain of parting once again. She looked around at the familiar buildings, trees, and grassy slope down to the creek. This had been her home for so many weeks that it was hard to leave. *I'll surely be* Heemweh *for them all,* she mused.

Jacob and Mary came along out to the van to say good-bye. Jacob was carrying a box, and he handed it to Nancy. "Here's a gift for you, for working for us this summer. We sure appreciated your help. I don't know what we'd have done without you."

Mary added, "You were such a help and a blessing to us. *Danki* for all you did."

"*Gern gschehne* (you're welcome). And *Danki* for this gift," Nancy replied. She wished she could think of something more to say.

"Take care of yourselves and the baby," Mom said in grandmotherly fashion.

Little Lydia was waving bye-bye as they pulled out the lane, and Nancy did the same. Mary and Susie waved until the van was out of sight.

Then at the end of Fishers' lane, Sally and Andrew were standing and waving their arms to say good-bye. Nancy waved back, for all she was worth, until her friends, too, disappeared from view.

"Good-bye, Summerville," Nancy whispered. "Hello, Whispering Brook Farm."

There was a deep peace in her heart, in spite of tender tuggings as they left Summerville. She was learning to accept the pain of parting with grace.

"Yes, I am growing up!" she whispered to herself. "And I'll be back for a visit someday."

"Let's sing," Henry suggested. "Sing the 'Good-bye Song.' I think we remember it well enough, don't we?"

"I don't know all the words," Nancy said. "But we can sing the chorus."

The van rang with their singing as they headed up through the mountains on their homeward way.

> Good-bye, good-bye,
> Dear friends, good-bye.
> If here we meet no more,
> Let's meet on heaven's shore.

The Author

The author's pen name is Carrie Bender. She is a member of an old order group. With her husband and children, she lives among the Amish in Lancaster County, Pennsylvania.